D1276419

indigo's star

ALSO BY HILARY McKAY

Saffy's Angel
Forever Rose
Permanent Rose
Caddy Ever After
Wishing for Tomorrow

MARGARET K. McELDERRY BOOKS

indigo's star

HILARY McKAY Margaret K. McElderry Books
New York   London   Toronto   Sydney

If you purchased this book without a cover, you should be aware
that this book is stolen property. It was reported as "unsold and
destroyed" to the publisher, and neither the author nor the
publisher has received any payment for this "stripped book."

MARGARET K. McELDERRY BOOKS
An imprint of Simon & Schuster Children's Publishing Division
1230 Avenue of the Americas, New York, New York 10020
This book is a work of fiction. Any references to historical events, real people,
or real locales are used fictitiously. Other names, characters, places, and
incidents are products of the author's imagination, and any resemblance to
actual events or locales or persons, living or dead, is entirely coincidental.
Copyright © 2003 by Hilary McKay
Originally published in Great Britain in 2003 by Hodder Children's Books
All rights reserved, including the right of reproduction
in whole or in part in any form.
MARGARET K. MCELDERRY BOOKS is a trademark of Simon & Schuster, Inc.
For information about special discounts for bulk purchases,
please contact Simon & Schuster Special Sales at 1-866-506-1949
or business@simonandschuster.com.
The Simon & Schuster Speakers Bureau can bring authors
to your live event. For more information or to book an event,
contact the Simon & Schuster Speakers Bureau at 1-866-248-3049
or visit our website at www.simonspeakers.com.
Also available in a Margaret K. McElderry Books hardcover edition
Book design by Kristin Smith
The text for this book is set in Melior.
Manufactured in the United States of America
1012 OFF
First Margaret K. McElderry Books paperback edition February 2006
8 10 9 7
The Library of Congress has cataloged the hardcover edition as follows:
McKay, Hilary.
Indigo's Star / Hilary McKay.—1st U.S. edition
p.   cm.
ISBN 978-0-689-86563-3 (hc)
Sequel to: Saffy's angel.
Summary: Spurred on by his younger sister, Rose, twelve-year-
old Indigo sticks up for himself and an American boy who has
replaced him as the primary target of the school bullies.
[1. Bullies—Fiction. 2. Brothers and sisters—Fiction. 3. Friendship—Fiction.
4. Family life—Fiction. 5. England—Fiction.] I. Title.
PZ7.M4786574In 2004
[Fic]—dc21 2003009941
ISBN 978-1-4169-1403-7 (pbk)

To Rachel Kearsey
Always a star!
With love from Hilary McKay

Chapter One

FOR THE FIRST TIME IN HIS LIFE INDIGO CASSON HAD BEEN properly ill. He had flu, and instead of getting better, it got worse and turned into infectious mononucleosis.

"Mono?" asked his disbelieving classmates. "Or scared stiff?"

Somewhere, at the back of his head, Indigo wondered the same thing. However, it really was mono. He grew very ill indeed, quite quickly. Even at the worst of his illness though, a part of Indigo sighed with relief. A part of him thought, Phew!

At first it was quite exciting for his family, having Indigo so ill. Anyone who asked any of the Cassons, "How's Indigo?" received a very long answer. A much too long answer, with lots of details most people would rather not know about.

Luckily, this stage did not last very long. Indigo's illness stopped being news and became a fact of life.

When people said, "How's Indigo?" his family answered, "Fine," and talked of more interesting things. This was not because they did not care about him, but just that there was nothing new to say. Anyway, compared to how he had been, Indigo was fine. He could walk up and down the stairs again. He could eat. He didn't keep fainting. He was fine.

Meanwhile, Indigo missed a whole term of school and grew extremely tall and thin. He spent a great deal of time by himself. The house was very quiet during the day. Caddy, his elder sister, was away at college. Eight-year-old Rose and Saffron (his adopted sister) were at school. His father and mother, both artists, were busy with their work, his father in London, and his mother in her shed at the end of the garden. It was a peaceful time, but it gave Indigo an odd feeling sometimes. As if, when he was alone, he became invisible. Once he looked in the mirror and grinned at himself and said, "Still there!"

Some days Saffron brought him work home from school. Other times Indigo read books or watched TV. Even so, he had hours and hours, especially at the start of getting better, when all he did was lie stretched out on his bed, dreamily watching the sky. He especially liked the clear days, when airplanes traveled across the blue, unfurling white banners of jet trails behind them. Indigo imagined them, full of people he did not know, journeying to places he had never seen. Even when the planes were too high to see, the jet trail banners listed their journeys across the sky.

Indigo thought that until he had become ill he had been on a journey of his own. Not a plane journey, but still a journey. He had been a traveler through the days and weeks and years of time.

Toward the end, Indigo's journey had become rather an unpleasant trip. Indigo's time of peaceful invisibility was brought to an end by Rose. Rose had a habit of pouncing on the phone at the first ring. One day she pounced, and it was her father, Bill Casson, calling from London. Far away, in his immaculate studio, Bill Casson heard a series of bumps. Bump, bump, bump, and then a thud.

"What on earth is that I can hear?" he asked, and Rose replied, "Indigo."

"Whatever was happening to him? Has he hurt himself?"

"He was just jumping down the stairs."

"Jumping down the stairs?"

"Yes."

"Jumping?"

"Yes."

"Then he must be better," said Bill.

Later on, when Rose reported this conversation, everyone looked at Indigo. It was true. He was better. Without anyone noticing, without noticing himself, he had got well again. His journey through the days and weeks and years of time was about to start once more. Indigo could hardly remember where he had been going in those far-off, before illness, six-inch-shorter days.

Eve, Indigo's mother, said happily, "You *are* better, Indigo darling! You will be able to go back to school!"

"Yes," said Indigo, and Rose wailed, "He still looks terrible to me!" and everyone laughed.

Only Rose in the whole family knew what going back to school must mean to Indigo. Saffron guessed a little, but Rose knew it all, or thought she did. There was a boy in her class who had a brother in Indigo's school. A long time ago this boy had told Rose what it was like for Indigo at school.

4

Just before he became ill, Rose had confronted Indigo with her information. Indigo had said angrily, "None of that is true! You shouldn't go listening to such lies!"

Rose was very hurt. Indigo had never been angry with her before. He had never lied to her either, and she knew he was lying now. She never mentioned it again, but she thought about it often.

Now she said remorsefully to Indigo, "You wouldn't have to go back if I hadn't told Daddy about you jumping down the stairs."

Indigo laughed and said, "Try your glasses on, Rose!" to make her think of something else. It was Sunday evening, and Rose's family had been attempting to get her to try her glasses on all week- end. Now, because she felt so guilty about Indigo going back to school, she went and fetched them. She put them on in front of everyone: Caddy, who was home for a weekend visit; Indigo; Saffron; and Sarah, Saffron's best friend, who spent so much time at the Casson house she was really one of the family.

"What do I look like, then?" asked Rose.

"You look fine," said Indigo.

"I only asked. I don't care."

5

"You look really cool," Caddy told her.

"And older," said Saffron.

"You look just right," added Sarah, doing her bit to help. "Cute!"

"Cute!" repeated Rose in disgust. "Me!"

Rose was wearing glasses for the first time ever, and because she was not used to them they began to do terrible things to her. She took a step forward and fell over a chunk of air. She stood still and the whole world came rushing toward her. When she put up her arms to protect herself, she hit Sarah in the face.

"All right! I'm sorry I said you looked cute!" exclaimed Sarah, reversing her wheelchair as Rose began to grope her way across the kitchen. "I meant gorgeous! Amazing! Clever! Bright . . . Open your *eyes*, Rose!"

"It's awful with my eyes open!"

"You don't need glasses," said Saffron. "You need radar!"

"It's Daddy's fault!" said Rose crossly. It was Rose's father who had discovered that Rose needed glasses, and on his last visit home he had taken her to the optician's and ordered them himself. He had chosen them,

6

too, with no help from Rose, who had been sulking at the time.

"I can see *too much*!" she complained, pulling the glasses off. "They must have gone wrong! That's better!"

"They just need getting accustomed to," said Sarah. "Like when I got my new wheelchair. I used to crash into people all the time."

"You still do," said Saffron, Caddy, and Indigo all together.

"Hardly ever. Only when I have to."

"Come over here," said Caddy to Rose, and steered her across the room. "Put them on again! There! Look!"

Rose looked and found she could see a very plain child watching her through a small bright window that had suddenly appeared in the kitchen wall.

"See," said Caddy. "I told you they looked cool!"

Then Rose's mind did a somersault, like a slow loop-the-loop in the sky, and the child in the window resolved itself into her own face reflected in the kitchen mirror.

"Oh!" she exclaimed, outraged. "Horrible, *horrible* Daddy!"

Indigo said quickly, "You don't look like that in real life!"

"I must!"

"You don't. No one looks like they really are, in mirrors. I'll show you. . . ." Indigo came and stood beside her so that he, too, was reflected. "There! Does that look like me?"

"Yes."

"It doesn't!"

"It does."

"Come into the garden and try them there," said Indigo.

Rose cheered up as she followed Indigo outside. It was nighttime. There was a cold spring wind blowing, and windy weather always made her a little light-headed. Also it was reassuring to see that even with her new glasses on, the garden looked much as it usually did, empty and shabby and lumpy with neglected grass. She gave a sigh of relief.

"It's a very starry night tonight," commented Indigo.

Indigo had perfect eyesight. He was nearly thirteen years old, and he had known the stars for years, but even he had to say, "Gosh! I've never seen so many!"

Rose had the sort of eyes that manage perfectly

well with things close by, but entirely blur out things far away. Because of this even the brightest stars had only appeared as silvery smudges in the darkness. In all her life Rose had never properly seen a star.

Tonight there was a sky full.

Rose looked up, and it was like walking into a dark room and someone switching on the universe.

The stars flung themselves at her with the impact of a gale of wind. She swayed under the shock, and for a time she was speechless, blown away by stars.

After a while Indigo fetched out the hearth rug for her so she could lie flat on the grass. Later on Caddy brought blankets. Saffron, who had walked Sarah home, came out to the garden when she returned and said, "But you've seen pictures of stars, Rose! You must have always known they were there!"

"I didn't," said Rose.

More time passed.

"They're in patterns, aren't they?"

"Yes," said Indigo.

"Some of them move."

"Those are airplanes, crossing the sky."

Later still, Rose said, "There's us. And then stars. Nothing in between. Except space."

"Yes."

"Indy?"

"Mmmm?"

"Aren't you scared of having to go back to school tomorrow?"

Rose and Indigo were the two youngest of the Casson family. Saffron was fourteen, and Caddy, the eldest, was nineteen. Caddy was home for the weekend, partly for Indigo's sake, because of going back to school, and partly in honor of Rose's new glasses. Caddy often came home, but the children's father did not. He preferred his studio in London, where he lived the life of a respectable artist, unburdened by family.

"He comes home on weekends," said Rose's mother.

"He doesn't," said Rose.

"Nearly every weekend, when he can fit it in."

"Only once since Christmas."

"Well, Daddy has to work very hard, Rose darling."

"So do you."

"Daddy is a proper artist," said Eve, which was

how she had always explained the difference between herself and Bill to the children. "A proper artist. He needs peace and quiet. . . . Anyway . . ."

"Anyway what?"

Eve gave Rose a painty hug and said she had forgotten what she was trying to say.

Eve did not have a studio, but she did not mind. She was perfectly happy in the garden shed, with the old pink sofa and a kitchen table someone had given her and various lamps and heaters that shot out frightening blue flames. Here she painted pictures of anything that would sell. She was very good at pets and children. People would give her photographs, and from them Eve would create astonishing portraits. Angelic glowing pictures of pets that looked human and intelligent (like children), and children who looked wistful and beguiling (like pets). Some families were beginning to collect whole sets.

"They are not exactly Art, Eve darling, are they?" Bill had commented reprovingly on his last visit home. He was looking at a particularly radiant picture, labelled *Pontus, Adam, and Katie*. "What do you think, Rose?"

Rose, who was an artist herself and had her own private opinion of her mother's portraits (megagross, especially Pontus, Adam, and Katie, who appeared to be floating through pastel-colored clouds), said that she thought her mother's paintings were brilliant, much better than his rotten pictures.

Rose's father hated scenes. So he smiled and said, "Of course they are much better than my rotten pictures! Aren't you fierce, Rosy Pose?" and tickled Rose's neck and pretended not to notice when he almost got his hand bitten.

Rose was not fierce at all the night she and Indigo lay in the windy garden looking at the stars. She said, "Perhaps everything will be different this term. Better."

"Yes. It will be fine."

"At my school no one bullies anyone. If you're mad with someone you just put their coats on the wrong peg. Or say, 'Ner, ner, ner! Bugs in your hair!' if you are really, really angry."

"Has anyone ever said that to you?"

"No. If they did, I'd just cross my fingers. Bounces back if you cross your fingers. So they get the bugs."

"Mmm?"

"Not everyone knows that."

Indigo laughed.

A shooting star fell like a dropped splinter of crystal, scratching a curve of silver across the sky.

"Make a wish!" said Indigo.

Rose made a wish, and then asked, "Why?"

"That's what I always do. Wish on the moving ones."

"Does it matter how fast they move?"

"I don't think so."

"Can you wish on airplanes, too?"

"Oh yes."

Rose wished on airplanes until she almost fell asleep, and then their mother was at the door calling, "Come in, Rose and Indigo, before you freeze!" and then it was bedtime, and then it was morning.

Chapter Two

INDIGO AWOKE WITH A STRANGE FEELING OF DOOM hanging over him. It was a minute or two before he realized what it was. Monday.

His school clothes were draped across a chair, black and shadowy gray. Their outlines became more and more clear as behind the closed bedroom curtains the light grew brighter. Footsteps and voices began to sound. Doors and floorboards creaked and rattled. Someone shouted, "Bathroom's empty."

Morning was now an unavoidable fact.

Indigo's bedroom door was pushed open, and Rose appeared saying, "It's the day. Are you awake?"

"Yes."

"I brought you this. Dad's mobile. I found it and I kept it for you. So you could ring for help. If you get bashed up again."

"I told you ages ago, I didn't get bashed up!"

"They stuck your head in a toilet," said Rose, who

was never at her most tactful in the mornings. "So I call that bashed up. Can I borrow something to wear?"

"Help yourself," said Indigo, and he watched as Rose rifled through the heap of clothes at the bottom of his bed. She emerged with an ancient black sweatshirt. It had chewed-up cuffs and came down to her knees.

"Perfect," she said, and disappeared, leaving the door open.

From all around came the sounds of the family preparing for the day. Caddy, on the telephone to some friend from college: "No, no, of *course* not a gorilla. You misheard. A chinchilla . . . Stop shouting! . . . A tiny little chinchilla . . . You will hardly notice it's there . . ."

Eve to Rose: "Darling, *that's* not school uniform."

"I know I know I know I know I know."

Hammering at the back door, followed by voices. Saffron talking to Sarah. Sarah shouting from the kitchen, "Where are you, Indy?"

"Coming," called Indigo.

By the time he arrived downstairs everyone was busy. Caddy and Rose were writing at the table. Eve was making porridge and at the same time dabbling a handful of painty brushes in a jar of turpentine.

Saffron was dictating homework answers to Rose. Everyone was tripping over Sarah's wheelchair, which was not folded up properly, and a large, sticky oil painting of a spaniel that was refusing to dry.

"It *has* to dry," said Eve, "because it has to be delivered today. It's a birthday present. Hello, Indigo darling. Look at this picture and tell me what you think."

"It looks really good."

"Bouncy?" asked Eve, scraping away in the porridge saucepan.

"More thoughtful than bouncy."

"Oh well, so long as it doesn't look dead."

"Why?"

"Because it *is* dead. I only had photos and a bit of brown fur they cut off afterward. They were very fond of it. They paid me in advance. Oh dear, I have never known paint to dry so slowly."

"Stick it under the grill," suggested Sarah. "Like toast."

"No, no, Sarah darling," said Eve. "It would be much too hot. Don't worry. I'll think of something."

"Hair dryer?"

"Burned out," said Eve, beginning to dollop porridge into cereal bowls. "Never mind. I'll put the oven

16

on and open the door when I have got everyone off to school. And waft it . . . There's your breakfast, Rose!"

"It looks just like hot concrete," observed Rose. "I've got to describe a day in the life of an Ancient Egyptian. What shall I put?"

"Is this your holiday homework?" asked Sarah. "Don't do it, Rose! Eve will write you a note to say it's iniquitous to give eight-year-olds homework in the school holidays! You will, won't you, Eve?"

"I could never spell 'iniquitous,' Sarah darling!"

"Hot concrete," said Rose mournfully, prodding her porridge.

"Write this," ordered Saffron. "'The Ancient Egyptians are all dead. Their days are very quiet.' Porridge is meant to look like hot concrete. Eat it up."

"Full of vitamins," remarked Eve hopefully, scratching another gluey chunk out of the saucepan and shaking it into a bowl. "Breakfast, Indy! Slice a banana on it! Caddy, pass him a banana! Any mail, does anyone know?"

"Daddy never writes," said Rose. "Ever. Never ever."

"Read the next question!" ordered Saffron.

17

"What would you say to Tutankhamen if you bumped into him in the street?"

"'Sorry!'" said Sarah at once. "Put that."

"We have to answer in proper sentences."

"'Sorry, but it was your fault! You were walking sideways!' Can I have a banana, too, please, Caddy?"

Caddy, who was trying to write a very difficult letter, passed Sarah a banana and read aloud:

"'Darling, darling Peter . . .'"

"Is it sensible to call him 'darling'?" interrupted Saffron.

"He would notice if I didn't."

"But he is *supposed* to notice. How can you dump him without him noticing?"

"I'm not dumping him. Not exactly. Listen. 'Darling, darling Peter . . .' I can't not call him that. 'I am really sorry I did not get to see you again. I was . . .' What can I say I was?"

"Out every night with Michael?" suggested Saffron.

"No!" said Caddy. "Anyway, I wasn't. Not every night. Eat up your porridge, Indigo, it's fantastically good for you. Help me with this letter, someone!"

"Tell the truth," advised Sarah. "It is kindest in the end. Put 'Dear Peter, I was just trying you out because I am trying out a lot of boyfriends. As many as possible in order to make sure that Michael is the one for me. I hope you will soon stop loving me. Yours sincerely, Cadmium Casson.' Michael *is* the one for you! You might as well face it, Caddy!"

"Michael is perfect," remarked Eve, and nobody disagreed. None of them could imagine life without Michael anymore. He had become one of the family. Caddy had adored him (and told him so) the first time she met him. "Darling!" she had exclaimed (loving his earring and his ponytail and his glancing black eyes), and Michael had replied, "Don't call me darling, I'm a driving instructor!"

For more than a year, while he heroically attempted to teach Caddy to drive, Michael had repeated these words, but each time with less conviction. He had known all along that they were meant for each other.

"Like Romeo and Juliet," Caddy had said happily.

"Crikey, I hope not!" Michael had said.

Despite (or maybe because of) being perfectly content with gorgeous Michael, Caddy could not resist dashing off from time to time in search of inferior comparisons.

Peter had been a very inferior comparison.

"Could I really put what Sarah said?" asked Caddy. "It's terribly tempting. . . . No, I can't! Let me get on. . . ."

"I never really managed to like Peter," said Eve. "I tried. But I couldn't help minding that he took a ten-pound note out of the housekeeping jam jar when he thought I wasn't looking. After all, he only had to ask. . . ."

"It was the way he tucked those little bits of hair behind his ears," remarked Sarah. "Both sides at once, and a little stroke afterward."

"He was here when my wobbly tooth came out," said Rose. "And he said was I going to put it under my pillow for the tooth fairy."

"*And* he was a bum patter," said Saffron.

"True," agreed Indigo.

Caddy gave Indigo a startled look, grabbed another piece of paper, and began to write very quickly.

"What *do* you do with your fallen-out teeth?" Sarah asked Rose.

"Grind them up for witch powder," said Rose calmly.

Sarah snorted with laughter and said, "Hurry up, Indy, or we'll miss the bus."

"I'm walking," said Indigo.

"Oh, *Indy*!"

"I don't mind walking, and the bus takes ages, going all around the streets like it does."

"But look at the rain!"

"I like rain," said Indigo stubbornly, "and anyway I said I'd go with Rose."

Saffron and Sarah gave up. They had to catch the bus because of Sarah's wheelchair and also because of the huge bags of self-inflicted homework they insisted on dragging back each night. So they said good-bye to Eve, hugged Caddy, who would be gone by the time school was over, and handed over the packed lunch Sarah's mother had made for Indigo.

"She said to eat every bit," Sarah told him. "It's full of vitamins and protein and slow-release carbo-hydrates. She said. Stuff it in his bag, Saffy!"

"I will!" said Rose, grabbing, but she was too late. Saffron had reached into Indigo's school bag and dis-covered the mobile phone. She held it up, her eye-brows raised and questioning behind Eve and Indigo's backs.

"It's so he can ring for help," explained Rose in a fierce whisper. "If he gets bashed up like before."

"What do you mean, bashed up? Come outside with us and explain!"

"They were horrible to him," said Rose as she helped Sarah down the steps, while Saffy followed with the schoolbags. "He says it's not true, but I know it is. A boy in my school told me. They flushed him down a toilet."

"That gang in his class?"

Rose nodded. Sarah put her arms round her and murmured, "All right. I know who you mean. Me and Saffy'll kill them."

"It's no good killing them if they've already done it," pointed out Rose.

"We'll kill 'em *first*!" hissed Sarah, ferociously. "Come on, Saffy, or we'll miss the bus!"

By the time Indigo and Rose were ready to leave, the rain had steadied to a thin gray dampness. Just as they were going, Eve produced a spare packed lunch for Indigo, in case the first one should prove to be inadequate. Cold sausages and an orange and a packet of chocolate Easter eggs.

"You used to love them when you were little," said Eve, stowing the untidy package on top of Sarah's mother's immaculate lunch box. "Should you like me to come and meet you at the end of school, Indigo? Just sort of casually, as if I were passing?"

"No! Really, Mum, please no!"

"I could make it look like an accident."

Indigo looked at Caddy for help.

"It would be dreadful," said Caddy firmly to Eve. "You musn't. Promise you won't."

"All right," agreed Eve, sighing. "You'd better go then, both of you. Rose darling, have you forgotten your new glasses? I thought I saw them in the cupboard a minute ago. Stuffed behind the jam."

"Did you?"

"Yes. Here they are! You wouldn't like to take them with you?"

"I KNEW," said Rose, in a loud, cross voice, "I KNEW SOMEONE WOULD TRY TO MAKE ME TAKE THOSE HORRIBLE GLASSES TO SCHOOL!"

Eve hastily stuffed them back behind the jam.

"They will be safe there," said Rose in her normal voice. "Come on, Indigo!"

Rose's school was only a few hundred yards away from the one that Indigo and Saffron and Sarah attended. Eve and Caddy watched as they trudged off together. Eight-year-old Rose looked very small beside Indigo's lanky new length.

"She's looking after him," said Caddy, and even as she spoke they saw Rose's hand reach out protectively to steer Indigo around a puddle.

Caddy was the last of the family to leave. She was being collected, she explained to her mother, by someone called Derek-from-the-camp.

"Is Derek the one after Peter?" enquired Eve, anxious to keep track.

"After Peter, but parallel to Michael," said Caddy. "You will love him. In fact . . . never mind! Here he is now!"

A large mud-covered figure on a magnificent (but also mud-covered) motorbike had pulled up outside. Very soon he was in the house, where he shook hands politely with Eve. He was, she noticed worriedly, much older than Caddy. Still, he was very charming. While Caddy collected her things, he drank scalding hot coffee in one unflinching swallow, beguiled Eve into signing a petition banning the activities of people she had never heard of, admired the sticky spaniel painting, and wrote down the name of a spray that

Eve could buy which would harden it enough to allow it to be packed. Finally he produced a newspaper from his pocket, demanded to know the star signs of each member of the family, and then read out wonderful horoscopes for each of them in turn.

Eve hugged him and Caddy good-bye quite happily and went off to spend the morning painting. The shed at the end of the garden was Eve's favorite place in the world. It was wonderfully quiet.

Chapter Three

AT SCHOOL THE NOISE HIT INDIGO LIKE A GALE. HE HAD completely forgotten the clatter and rumble of corridors. He had forgotten the school smell. He had almost forgotten the routine of the day. He had to remind himself, *Find your locker*.

Because the school was overcrowded there were lockers situated in every available space: along corridors, at the backs of classrooms, in odd corners of entrances and bathrooms. The boys in Indigo's class had theirs in a room that also doubled as a changing room and bathroom. A line of coat pegs ran down the middle, dividing the room. It was chilly and damp-feeling, with a depressing smell of pine disinfectant, old clothes, and toilets.

"Not an entirely satisfactory arrangement," said the Head, who always skipped this part of the school when conducting tours of the building.

This unsatisfactory room was where every school day began and ended for Indigo. Also, it was the meeting place of the gang. The gang were his enemies, and had been ever since the first week of term at this new school, when he had interrupted them just as they had finally succeeded in hanging a fellow classmate from one of the high iron coat pegs by his twisted sweatshirt collar.

It was only a bit of harmless torture, pure routine. Indigo had been advised to stay cool. Nevertheless, he tried to interfere.

This meddling did no good to anyone. For a start, to punish Indigo, the boy (who later turned into an enthusiastic gang member and expert torturer himself) was kept in his uncomfortable position for much longer than he otherwise would have been. This caused him great discomfort. Also, it meant that for several minutes after he was at last cut down (ruining his sweatshirt), he bothered everyone by choking uncontrollably and writhing on the floor as though he were dying.

"Go and get someone to help him!" Indigo had yelled at this point (still not minding his own business), and one or two of the more faint-hearted spectators had to be forcibly restrained from carrying out his order. So they got hurt too.

Then the hanged boy revived enough to sit up and take notice, and the redheaded gang leader explained to him that all the trouble he had suffered was the direct result of Indigo's interference. The hanged boy was not stupid. He agreed at once that this was obviously true.

Indigo did not take in that the gang leader and the hanged boy were now on the same side. Also, despite having had both arms twisted with excruciating efficiency behind his back during the whole hanging, writhing, choking episode, he still had not learned when to keep quiet.

"You should tell someone!" he foolishly advised the hanged boy. "You should tell someone what they did to you! I'll come with you if you want me to. . . ."

"What's going on here?" demanded a teacher, barging in at that moment, right on time.

Indigo paused, waiting for the boy he had tried to rescue to speak for himself.

"Nothing," said the hanged one from his place on the floor, smiling and blinking like a cat in sunshine. "Nothing at all," he repeated, and was rewarded by a friendly hand from the redheaded gang leader, helping him to his feet.

"They nearly choked you!" shouted Indigo, who had been released when the teacher came in.

The hanged one had looked at Indigo as if he was something scraped up off the dirty tiled floor, rolled his eyes to the ceiling, leaned back on the redheaded gang leader's shoulder, and grinned.

"Relax, Indigo," he said.

"No need to get all hung up," someone added, and then there was a great roar of laughter all round, and the teacher said irritably, "Outside, all of you!" and the incident was over.

It was over, but not forgotten. Indigo had criticized the gang, interfered with their business, almost started a rebellion in the ranks (those faint-hearted ones who had wanted to run for help), and finally tried to tell on them to a teacher. From that time onward he was in the lonely (and often painful) position of gang enemy.

Even after a whole term away, Indigo was still gang enemy. He knew it as soon as he walked through the door. Last night in the garden suddenly seemed a long time ago.

The presence of this gang divided Indigo's class into two separate groups.

One contained nearly all the girls and a few non-descript boys. They were allowed to go their own way, half ignored and half protected. They paid for their protection with silence. That meant they took no notice of the activities going on all around them. In return no notice was taken of them.

The rest of the class were the gang members.

Quite a large part of them were nothing worse than a noisy rabble.

The rabble, when they were not clowning for survival, helped with the general pushing and shoving around of any chosen victims. This group was kept in order by the horrid and very real possibility of becoming victims themselves.

They were led by an inner circle of decision makers. Risk-takers, heartbreakers, please-don't-make-us-do-this-to-you fakers. All hand-picked by the red-haired gang leader. It was strange the power they had, considering how little they actually did. No heavy thumping or hanging or tripping up. No messy toilet dunking. Perhaps a little gentle taunting now and then.

"Hey, Indy! We thought you'd died!"

"You didn't die, did you Indy?"

"Feeling all right now, Indigo? Feeling good?"

It was the leader of the gang who said that, the redheaded boy with the startlingly white and bony face. He asked again, smiling menacingly, "Feeling good, Casson?"

Outside the window the sky was becoming lighter. The clouds were breaking up. A patch of blue showed. Indigo remembered Rose, wishing on airplanes.

"Yes, thank you," he said.

"Glad to be back?" The redheaded boy took a step nearer.

Indigo did not reply.

"Glad to be back, Casson?"

Indigo glanced at the door, calculating the distance.

"We asked," said the redheaded gang leader, with a quick look over his shoulder to check that his troops were in place, "if you were glad to be back, Casson."

Indigo thought that if he went home visibly

thumped, kicked, hung, or toilet dunked, Rose would not be able to bear it. The thought sickened him.

"Casson? Are. You. Gla—"

Indigo lifted his head and said, "No."

"You're *not* glad to be back?" repeated the red-headed leader, and the rabble gathered around began to hum with delight.

Suddenly Indigo had had enough. He needed to be out of this room, and he did not care very much how he got there. He began to push his way through the rabble. They closed together in front of him without seeming to move.

"Where do you think you're going, Casson?" asked the redheaded gang leader.

"Out."

"No, you're not."

"I am," said Indigo, continuing his stubborn progress toward the door.

The rabble began to buzz angrily. Something was going wrong. Little by little, Indigo was making his way forward, despite them. They looked toward their leaders for guidance, and the buzz grew louder. It was so loud it was heard in the corridor outside by Sarah and Saffron, who were not there by accident.

Sarah and Saffron shot into the room where no girl had set foot before, and they mowed down the rabble like bowling pins, Saffron with her knees and fists, and Sarah with her wheelchair.

Indigo yelled, "Saffy! Sarah! Get out!"

Sarah laughed, and Saffron said, "Shut up, Indigo!"

They headed straight for the white-faced, red-haired leader of the gang, bowling him backward into a porcelain sink on which he cracked his head.

Indigo shut his eyes and hoped he was having a terrible dream. He opened them, and there was the gang leader being hauled vertical again by a raging Saffron, while Sarah barred the door.

"Don't you dare," said Saffron, blazing like an angry comet, her fists twisted full of his orange hair, "*ever* touch my brother. Ever." Saffron jerked his head, her fingers gripping tight.

"Not you . . ."

(Jerk)

". . . or any of your gang. . . ."

(Jerk)

"Because if you do, me and Sarah . . ."

(Jerk, jerk)

". . . will *finish* you!"

Saffron gave a final yank and dropped him.

"Saffron," said Indigo into the appalled silence that filled the room. "Saffy. You didn't need to do that."

Saffron ignored him. She said, "Get out of my way," to the rabble, and they parted before her. They stared as she washed her hands. They saw red hair fill the plug hole of the hand basin.

Saffron dried her hands and looked around the room, memorizing faces. Sarah said, "I know all their names."

The room was completely quiet. Saffron and Sarah were the most noticeable girls in the school. Everyone knew Saffron with her long legs and long gold hair and legendary exam results. Everyone knew Sarah and the story of how she had been expelled from the private school of which her own mother was Head, after breaking every rule, deliberately, one a day, until the battle was finally over.

"See you later then, Indy," said Sarah, and swished out of the room, Saffron stalking after her. Nobody looked at Indigo, and nobody looked at the bony-faced leader of the gang, who was smoothing down what remained of his hair. Nobody spoke, but across the room somebody laughed.

It was a rude, loud, scornful laugh.

The bony-faced one stopped smoothing his hair and straightened up and looked. Indigo looked too. A dark-haired, brown-eyed boy, whom he had never seen before, was leaning against a wall, watching them. He was smaller than anyone else in the room, but he did not look like he knew this. He raised his eyebrows at Indigo, amused and contemptuous, and said, "Now I've seen everything." He told the red-haired (what was left of it) gang leader, "You lost that one, Baldy."

The red-haired gang leader knew he must re-establish his authority at once, or else it would be gone forever. He glanced briefly across to the rabble, checking his troops were still with him, and then looked coldly over to the boy who had called him "Baldy" and said, "Him."

The inner circle nodded.

Indigo felt a sudden weary feeling inside. He remembered when they had looked at him in just that way, and nodded, in that same way.

The rabble, however, relaxed into sudden happy

relief. For them order had been restored. The gang was still in power. Its leader was still its leader. And they were safe. They were still the comfortable rabble. There was a new victim.

The leaders were leaving the room. The rabble followed riotously, taking care to jostle the new victim on their way. In seconds his book bag was on the floor, and its contents kicked casually to the dampest parts of the tiled floor.

At first he seemed stunned by the suddenness with which they had turned on him. Then he began to shout and run at them, lunging from one kicker to another, but in moments the room was empty.

Only Indigo remained.

Indigo picked up the scattered books, wiped them as well as he could and unfolded the creased pages. He said, "You shouldn't have made them mad."

"*I* shouldn't have made them mad!" repeated the boy. "It was your crazy sister and her friend made them mad! Rescuing *you*!"

"I know. But they don't like being laughed at."

"This place stinks!"

"Yes," agreed Indigo. "Sometimes."

"Sometimes! This place stinks *forever*!"

"There's all your books. I think they are okay."

The boy rolled his eyes upward as if in disbelief, his look saying, *They are not okay*.

In the corridor outside, a bell rang. Indigo said, "We'd better go."

The boy took a rubber ball from a pocket and squeezed it hard. Then he bounced it against the tiled floor. He bounced and caught it, over and over, his face tight with anger.

Indigo said again, "We'd better go."

The boy bounced the ball, caught it, and flicked it hard at Indigo's head. It hit his cheekbone with a pain like a burn. In a moment the boy had caught the ball and thrown it again. This time it caught Indigo on the ear.

"Well, don't just stand there!" exclaimed the strange boy. "You just *stand* there! Why do you just *stand there*?"

"I don't know," said Indigo.

The ball came at him again. This time Indigo was ready and he caught it. He held it for a moment, then tossed it gently back to its owner.

"I'm not fighting you," he said. "Come on. We'll be late."

Chapter Four

AFTER CADDY HAD GONE, EVE MADE COFFEE IN THE QUIET kitchen and sat down at the table. There she found herself gazing at the artist's color chart on the kitchen wall. All the children's names had come from that chart. Cadmium Gold, Indigo, and Rose each had their own little blocks of color, and long ago another had been added for Saffron (Saffron Yellow). Saffron had been adopted into the family when she was three years old and her own mother, Eve's sister, had died.

"Darling Saffy," Eve said, looking at the little square of yellow.

Saffron was the only one who did not need worrying about.

All the others did, and in between phone calls and painting and trying to get the car to start, Eve spent the day doing just that, going from Caddy tearing back to London on the back of someone's motorbike, to Indigo who looked as thin as a paint-brush and as white as paper, and then on to Rose, who was permanently cross with her father.

Worrying about Rose's father, Eve had fallen asleep. She had stretched out on the old pink sofa that she kept in her shed, closed her eyes, and forgotten them all.

Rose was the first of the family to arrive home from school. She found the house unlocked but empty, no sound from anywhere, and the kitchen full of shadows. However, a light was shining in her mother's shed. Rose picked her way down the narrow garden path and peered in at the window.

Eve was still asleep, and Rose was disappointed. She would have liked a little company, but she knew from experience that it was no good trying to wake her mother. Eve, emerging from sleep, was a terrible nuisance. She flailed around with her eyes screwed shut, groping for coffee and knocking things over. She moaned "Darling, darling!" and walked into walls.

Asleep, her mother looked rather like Caddy, Rose thought. A blurry version of Caddy. Caddy

39

painted with not quite such good colors and a slightly worn brush.

"Caddy," said Rose aloud, already missing her. She tried to imagine Caddy in London, but she could not. London always seemed to belong to her father, who had rented a studio there since before she was born. Rose had never been to London, so she had never seen her father's studio, but she had seen the pictures he painted there. He brought them home sometimes, to show to the family.

"Darling, how wonderful," Eve would say whenever he produced a new one. "I don't know how you do it!" And Bill would be pleased, and know it was true, and she didn't know how he did it.

Caddy, Saffron, and Indigo made comments like, "Gosh, how huge!" and "Brilliant! As good as a photo!" and Bill, who had long ago decided they were immune to all forms of culture, did not mind a bit.

Then (unless she had managed to sneak off before her turn came) Rose's father would say tensely, "Rose? Painting here for you to criticize!"

"You always get mad, whatever I say."

"Just tell me what you think, Rose darling."

"Oh. Well. It's very nice."

"Rose!"

"I can see what it's meant to be."

Rose's father would bury his face in his hands.

"I didn't say I didn't like it!"

Then Caddy and Eve and Saffron and Indigo would all have to interfere and be tactful and point out that Rose was only eight and knew nothing about art. They were never very successful, and Rose's father was never very convinced. Everyone knew Rose had an unerring eye for perfection. Bill had tested her once with a catalog brought back from a gallery in Italy. "Which is the best?" he had asked her, and Rose had flipped back and forth through the pages and ended up with a drawing, a reddish, brownish sketch.

"Oh," said Bill, "Michelangelo." He had been quite depressed.

Rose's own pictures drove her father mad. She only used paper as a last resort. Like Michelangelo, she preferred walls. The desert landscape with red gloss highlights that she had painted on the upstairs landing when she was not quite seven years old still persisted in reappearing, despite three coats of magnolia emulsion. Right now, she had in production her biggest work to date. It was done in colored pastels on the kitchen wall, which was very handy for Rose because she could alter it whenever she wanted. It was a picture of her family sitting on the roof of their house, like animals on the top of a sinking ark.

Out in the garden, Rose watched her mother sleeping for a little while longer. Then she turned away and went back to the house and began to draw. She added extra gold to Caddy's hair, and closed her mother's eyes so that now she was asleep on the roof, slumped against the chimney. Dreaming, thought Rose, and sketched a fragile circle of dreamy purple smoke around her head.

Eve smiled, dreaming against the chimney pot.

Rose smiled back and began to draw herself in, close against Indigo, who was anchored very firmly in the middle of the roof, his feet resting in the guttering so that he could not possibly slip. She became so absorbed in this that she did not notice when Indigo walked in, until he came up right behind her and made her jump.

"Are you all right?" she demanded, flinging herself on him. "Was it as horrible as you thought it would be? Did they stick your head in the toilet again?"

"I was perfectly all right," Indigo told her, disentangling himself. "I told you I would be. Hey, look at your picture! I like Mum! What's happened to Dad?"

"He's behind that cloud," said Rose, pointing to a gray and thundery shape hovering low over the roof.

"Why?"

"I don't know," said Rose, sounding a bit forlorn. "I don't know why he does anything."

Indigo dropped the subject and began to unpack his school bag. "Look what Sarah's mum gave me for my lunch! Nuts and raisins and bananas! She must think I'm a monkey."

He did a few monkey steps to make Rose laugh, and she stopped drawing white lightning daggers shooting from her father's cloud and took a banana instead. While she ate, Indigo told her about the new boy who had appeared in his class.

"He's called Tom. Tom Levin. He's from America. He's staying over here until term finishes."

"Why does he have to do that?"

Tom had attracted a great deal of attention with his explanation of why he had happened to be in England. Also a great deal of ridicule, which had not caused him to change his story in the slightest.

"He said," began Indigo cautiously, "that his father is an astronaut. . . ."

"A *space* astronaut?"

"He just said an astronaut."

"Is he in space *now*?" asked Rose, looking out the window. "What about his mother? Is she an astronaut as well?"

"No. She does something else. She's away, too, Tom said. Looking after bears . . ."

"Looking after bears?"

"In Yellowstone National Park."

"Oh, Yellowstone," said Rose, nodding wisely, as if she went there often. "Yogi Bear lives there."

"So he's stopping over here with his English grandmother until school finishes. . . ."

"Then will he go and help his mother with the bears?"

"He didn't say."

"Or maybe his father will be back."

"Perhaps."

"Does he like it here?"

"I don't think so," said Indigo, remembering how the rabble had imitated everything Tom said all afternoon, and the way the red-haired gang leader had looked at him. He had looked at Tom in a way that stopped even the lucky ones in the ignored-but-protected group from attempting to make friends.

"I wonder if Daddy ever thought of being an astronaut," remarked Rose. "We could have gone and watched him being blasted off. Do you mind if I have some of your peanuts?"

"Help yourself! Hello, here's Saffy!"

Saffron came bouncing through the door looking very pleased with herself and asking, "Has Indigo told you how Sarah and I saved his life, Rose?"

"No, I haven't, and anyway, you didn't!" said Indigo. "And don't you ever come barging into our bathroom like that again! It was awful!"

"Had to be done!" said Saffron cheerfully. "And me and Sarah enjoyed it, if you didn't. It was lovely the way that boy's hair came out! It was terribly loose. I hardly had to twitch it."

"You told me you were fine at school, Indigo!" exclaimed Rose. "Perfectly all right, you said!"

"I was," said Indigo. "Perfectly. I promise I was."

"He was," Saffron told Rose. "You needn't start

worrying. Sarah and I just checked up on him, that's all. Where're your glasses? I promised Caddy I'd remind you."

"Well, you have reminded me."

"Where are they?"

Rose opened the cupboard door and pointed so that Saffy could see where her glasses were, barracked in a corner by a pot of apricot jam, gone moldy on the top.

"Are you going to leave them in there?"

"Yes. Unless there's any stars I need to look at." Rose suddenly remembered some news she had to tell. "Caddy telephoned while I was here on my own. She says she got back okay, and she's looking after someone's chinchilla. She's got it in her room. What's a chinchilla look like?"

"A sort of catty, rabbity, squirrelly, koala-beary thing," Saffron told her. "Where's Mum? I'm starving to death."

"She's in the shed," said Rose. "Asleep. So not cooking. I'm hungry too. I should like something hot."

In her picture a catty, rabbity, squirrelly, koala-beary thing had already begun to materialize on the roof beside Caddy. Saffron and Indigo watched in admiration as Rose rubbed silver highlights into its fur with spit and the corner of a tea towel.

"I should like soup," Rose remarked hungrily.

She finished the highlights, scratched in delicate curling whiskers with her fingernail, and added two bright reflections to the eyes. The chinchilla came suddenly to life, as all Rose's pictures did.

"Hot soup," said Rose, and began to shade in the deep water lapping around the walls of the family home.

Saffron and Indigo looked at each other and then out of the window toward the closed door of the shed. There was no sign of anyone hurrying out to prepare hot soup, or anything else for that matter.

"I suppose *we* could make soup," said Indigo doubtfully, "but it would take ages. And anyway we would need the stuff to make it with . . . vegetables and things. . . ."

Rose interrupted to explain that she meant proper soup, out of tins.

"Tins!" exclaimed Saffron, all at once remembering they had that very thing, tins of soup won by Sarah's mother in a raffle and donated to the Cassons the year before. It took a little while to find them among the enormous clutter of the Casson kitchen, but they were unearthed at last from behind a box of Christmas decorations.

In no time at all hopeful smells started to fill the air. Rose sniffed them happily and read the labels. "Minestrone. Lovely! Why didn't Sarah's mother want it?"

"She doesn't like stuff out of tins."

"What's the matter with stuff out of tins?"

"She says it's not proper cooking. Dad is just the same."

"Is he?"

"You must remember."

"Why do you think Daddy never comes home anymore?" asked Rose, and Saffron and Indigo looked at her in surprise.

"He comes home!" said Saffy at once. "Of course he comes home! Doesn't he, Indy?"

"Yes," said Indigo, although he did not speak quite as certainly as Saffron had done. "He does come home. Not as much as he used to. But he comes when we need him."

Rose snorted.

"He does rush home in an emergency," agreed

Saffron. "Sometimes he makes an awful fuss, but he always does it. Like he did to get your glasses, Rose."

"That wasn't an emergency."

"Well then, like when Indy had to go to hospital last term and have a blood transfusion. And when Caddy ran away from University after she'd only been there a week, because she was so homesick."

"And when the car got wheel-clamped and taken away and the guinea pig was still in the trunk," said Indigo. "He came home all those times."

"Those times were all ages ago," objected Rose. "Do you think he would come home *now* if we needed him to?"

"Of course he would," said Indigo and Saffron.

Rose thought about that on Tuesday evening when they had soup again, and on Wednesday, when the soup was all gone. That evening, on the way to the fish-and-chips shop, Eve's car hiccuped and stopped only a few hundred yards from home. Rose and her mother, who had climbed in with high hopes only a minute or two before, climbed out again very dejectedly and plodded home. There it soon became apparent that the only possible hot food was baked potatoes.

"Daddy is the one who is good at supermarkets," said Eve apologetically as she switched on the oven. "Never mind, Rose, you like baked potatoes."

This was true, and Rose tried not to think about the endless hungry time that would have to pass between the potatoes being put in the oven and them being taken out again, ready to eat. She occupied a part of it by writing to her father.

Darling Daddy,

Poor Saffy. She had a big fight in the boys toilets on Monday, did you know? A very big fight and Sarah helped and it was terrifying. Said a boy in my class who has a brother who was there.

Rose was not at all sure that Indigo and Saffron were correct when they agreed that their artistic but absent father could be relied upon to rush home in times of crisis, but she thought it was worth a try.

Saffy washed her hands and said Never Ever Never Dare You Touch My Brother. (Indigo). And the plug holes were blocked with hair.

Love from Rose.

Rose read it through and decided it needed something more, a homely touch, so that it was not all crisis. She looked around the kitchen for inspiration and then added another few lines.

Sarah's mother has given us soup. Soup soup soup and then it was all gone.

L.F.R.

She scribbled a row of kisses across the bottom of the page, found a stamp and an envelope, addressed it, and pushed her letter inside, hammering the stamp down hard with her fist.

"I'm going to mail something," she announced through the sitting room door, and hurried away before anyone could say, "Not on your own, darling!"

On the way to the mailbox Rose did calculations. Today was Wednesday. Her letter would arrive on Thursday. Her father, she hoped, would be home by Friday at the latest. Then her mother would stop painting portraits of dead animals and come out of her shed, the car would be fixed, the cupboard shelves restocked, and most important, a way would be found to keep Indigo safe at school.

"And I will show him my picture on the kitchen wall," said Rose aloud. Right after Indigo was sorted out, even before she showed him the empty cupboard shelves.

"Not on your own, darling," said Eve as Rose re-entered the house.

"I've been," said Rose.

Chapter Five

SAFFRON AND SARAH'S ENERGETIC ENCOUNTER WITH THE red-haired gang leader left him with two difficulties.

The first was that it hurt to comb his hair. He stopped combing it. That was one problem solved.

The second difficulty was that (for the moment) Indigo could not be touched. Another encounter with Saffron and Sarah was too horrible to contemplate. The leader's subtle and resourceful brain went to work on this complication, but it did not bother him for very long. There were so many things that could happen at school which Indigo would not enjoy.

One of them had started already.

Everyone knew how squeamish Indigo was when being forced to witness the antics of the gang with a victim. It was easy to arrange that he should see some more. It was not even necessary to sacrifice one of the rabble to do so. Right on time, someone new had arrived. Tom, withering and scornful, asking for trouble.

At first it was hard for the red-haired gang leader to turn the rabble from Indigo to Tom. They were not a very intelligent bunch. Over and over again they had to be patiently reminded, "Not him! *Tom!* Over there!" It was a bit like training dogs.

Indigo always hurried to defend Tom when the dogs were urged into action, but he soon found he was of very little use. He had become invisible again. When he hurled himself at the crowd as they shoved and jostled Tom, they parted before him, but closed up at once behind. They were deaf to his shouts. They did not seem to feel any pain when he hammered on their backs. The bony-faced red-haired leader smiled gently through him, as if he were a gap in a wall.

That first week of term Tom's possessions became more battered by the day, but inexplicably, Tom did not. No matter how outnumbered he was, he always fought back. He refused to be a victim, and it soon became apparent that he was the most difficult person the gang had ever undertaken to bully. The rabble had to be continually reminded to do their duty. Their leader had never had to work so hard. Part of his problem was that Tom would not stop talking.

Indigo listened to Tom talking, and he did not know what to think. Obviously, he realized, Tom talked because he liked to be listened to. He liked an audience, any audience, even an audience of enemies, as long as they paid attention.

Nothing could have been more detached, more reasonable, more self-assured than Tom's way of telling his unbelievable stories.

"Your dad's an astronaut, right, Tom?" someone would ask.

"Right," Tom agreed lazily.

"An astronaut, you said?"

"At the moment."

"What d'you mean, 'at the moment'?"

"Well, obviously he wasn't *always* an astronaut. You're not *born* an astronaut."

Then there would be a pause. Rabble members, ignored-but-protecteds, and casual hangers-on would consult together. Obviously, a person was not born an astronaut. Did he think they were stupid?

A new questioner emerged and took over.

"What was he before?"

"Baseball player."

Nobody in Tom and Indigo's class, nobody in the

entire school, knew anything about baseball players, but still, it sounded improbable.

"Liar."

Tom shrugged.

"You mean a *good* baseball player?"

Tom always seemed to have a rubber ball about him somewhere. He took one out of his pocket and began tossing it from hand to hand, but the questions persisted.

"You mean a *proper* baseball player?"

Tom bounced his ball off the ceiling, caught it, and glanced with raised eyebrows at the questioner. His glance asked the world, "What kind of a fool is this?"

"You mean a *professional* baseball player?"

Tom lost interest and drifted away, still bouncing his ball off the ceiling. He left behind him a trail of small circular gray marks high above his head, and a whole crowd of people saying, "What a liar! What a *total* liar!"

"Who is a liar?" demanded the red-haired gang leader, walking through Indigo as if he were fog. "Who?"

"Tom."

"Levin? Tom Levin? Yes," said the gang leader virtuously. "Yes. He's a liar."

Tom did no work at all in class. Nothing. If he was asked a question, he shrugged and replied, "Who knows?" His watchful, scornful brown eyes said, even more plainly, "Who cares?"

Sometimes he would take his ball out of his pocket and drop and catch it from hand to hand. The drops would start off very small, and the catches would be hardly a movement. Almost imperceptibly, however, they grew bigger. Tom's chair would tilt back to give himself extra space. He made the game more interesting by catching the drops with his eyes shut. Then he would go for a bounce.

Bounces were more than any teacher could put up with for long, and sooner or later Tom would be sent out of the room. He always went willingly. Inside the classroom they would hear the bounces of his ball, more and more faintly, as he wandered away.

On Thursday afternoon Derek-from-the-camp turned up at the Casson house. He happened to be passing, he said, and had stopped off to say hello. Rose arrived home at just the same time, and in a moment of inspiration she asked him, "Are you any good at fixing cars?"

Derek turned out to be spectacularly good at fixing cars, and he cured the Casson one almost immediately with the simple but highly effective addition of gasoline.

"I knew there was something I was meaning to buy!" exclaimed Eve, delighted to hear the good news.

"Now you *can* go shopping," said Rose.

"Oh yes," said Eve, unenthusiastically.

Indigo and Saffron arrived back from school to find her busy with a shopping list, while Rose rewarded Derek's car-fixing skills by adding his portrait to the collection of people in her picture on the kitchen wall.

"Hello, Saffy. Hello, Indigo," said Eve. "Batteries, turpentine, hair dye . . . Don't talk to me! I'm trying to think! Darling Derek has mended the car!"

Derek's glance went upward, a little surprised, and Rose said severely, "She calls everyone darling! Keep still!"

"I *don't* call everyone darling!" protested Eve. "Do you need any more pastels, Rose?"

"Yes, please. I always need more."

"Batteries, turpentine, hair dye, pastels for Rose.

Some flowers would be nice, those big pink lilies. . . . What else should we buy?"

"Food," said Saffron sternly.

Eve gave a big sigh and asked, "What sort of food?"

"Things for breakfast," said Rose immediately. "Things for supper, things for in between, Diet Coke and coffee to keep you awake, and stuff Daddy likes in case he comes home tomorrow."

"Oh, Rose," said her mother. "Daddy would have said by now if he was coming home tomorrow."

There was a little silence while everyone looked at Rose. Rose did not say anything, but she stopped drawing Derek and instead began sketching very rapidly near the bottom of her picture. In no time at all the deep water that lapped the walls of the house was filled with the dorsal fins of cruising sharks.

"Rose," said Derek, watching her, "you are absolutely fantastic at drawing."

Rose gave him a quick sideways look to see if he was making fun of her. He wasn't, she decided, and she began to like him very much.

"Derek," said Saffron, asking something they had all wondered about, "what do you do in your camp?"

"Write my thesis. Book," he added for Rose's sake. "Write my book."

"Gosh. In a tent?"

"Up on the moors. Bronze Age sites all over up there. Stone circles, standing stones. Unfortunately there's also a great big quarrying company that wants to take out all the side of the hill from underneath."

"From underneath?" asked Indigo.

"Yep."

"Then won't everything on top just fall down?"

"Too true everything on top will fall down," said Derek, grinning. "That's why we are there. We're a protest camp!"

Later, when he had gone, and Eve had driven away to the shops, Rose asked Indigo, "What do protest camps do?"

"They protest," explained Indigo. "They make a fuss about things they think are wrong. Instead of just putting up with them."

"Oh," said Rose. "Well, I know something you should make a fuss about because that boy in my class who's got a brother in your class told me—"

"I don't want to know what he said!" Indigo interrupted crossly. "You stop listening to that boy!"

"I was only going to say you and Tom could have a protest camp!"

Indigo glanced out of the window at the steady rain, and he could not help laughing.

"Derek has one," pointed out Rose, but she had to add fairly, "That's why he's always covered in mud."

"I think he comes here to get warmed up," remarked Saffron. "Have that boy and his gang been bothering you again, Indigo?"

"No," said Indigo.

"They'd better not! I didn't know you and Tom were friends."

Indigo almost began to say that neither did he, and then thought a little further. Perhaps they might be friends. They were definitely on the same side, anyway. Why shouldn't they be friends?

"Why shouldn't we be friends?" he said aloud to Saffy.

"No reason at all," said Saffy cheerfully.

Indigo went into school on Friday with this thought in mind.

All that morning the weather got worse and worse, until by lunchtime it was so bad that no one could be sent outside. Indigo's class, who were considered to be a particularly pleasant and responsible group of students, were told they would be allowed to stay unsupervised in their classroom until the afternoon lessons began.

Almost the whole class was gathered together by the time Indigo finished his lunch and came to the room. As soon as he walked through the door he realized that trouble was coming. The red-haired gang leader was watching out for him. Indigo, as he was meant to do, caught the quiet words, "Not him. Levin," as he came into the room.

Indigo looked quickly around for Tom. He was over by a window, entertaining an audience as usual. He looked very much in control, flicking a ball across the room to a random selection of rabble members, and deftly catching it every time it came flying back.

"You miss that ball and it will go right through the window," the red-haired gang leader told him.

"As if you care," said Tom, eyebrows raised in scorn, and threw it at his head. The red-haired gang leader caught it and threw it carefully back, as if he really did care. Tom, looking annoyed, stuffed the ball in his pocket. Obviously, he did not consider the game worth playing if there was no risk of broken glass.

Indigo began to relax, now that the ball was safely out of the way. One of the rabble, not wanting the entertainment to stop so soon, called out, "Hey, Tom, tell us about your mother! How're the bears getting on?"

Tom shrugged irritably, crossed the room, and banged himself down at a table. Just as he did so, right under Indigo's nose, the red-haired gang leader reached out and twitched his chair away.

Tom sat down on nothing with a sickening thump, and the room erupted with laughter.

Tom groaned. With a face the color of wet paper, he doubled up and retched, knocking his forehead against his knees. Indigo dropped beside him and grabbed his shaking shoulders. He said urgently, "Don't try to move! Put your head down!"

Tears of anger and pain streamed down Tom's face.

"Kiss him better, Indigo," said the red-haired gang leader.

"Run and fetch your sister," suggested someone else.

Tom struggled free from Indigo's grasp and tottered upright. He looked around and he tried twice, but he could not speak. Lurching from table to table for support, he began to stumble toward the door. Indigo hurried in front of him, clearing a path through the sniggering rabble and guiding him out of the room.

Nobody followed as they made their way down the back stairs and along a corridor. Tom was white and sweaty and he walked silently, as if he were alone.

They came to a small service door that led outside, to the back of the school. Tom swayed against it, and after a moment, pushed it open. Indigo followed him outside and watched as he stood leaning against a wall, gulping the rainy air.

"What do you want to do?" he asked, when at last Tom began to breathe more easily. "I'll go home with you if you like. Or go and find a teacher to help you."

"Leave me alone. I don't want anyone."

"I can't just leave you alone."

Tom shrugged and turned away.

They were in the back playground, one of the most dismal parts of the school, and the gray wet day made it seem even worse. On one side stood the cafeteria and kitchens. Beside them was an old fire escape, a metal spiral staircase that came down from an upstairs door. It was chained off across the bottom step, and strictly forbidden. Tom made his way across to it and began painfully to climb the chains. The rain came down suddenly hard, turning the back of his gray T-shirt black all in a moment.

Indigo saw Tom's shoulders flinch and then begin to shake.

"Here," he said, and pulled off his jacket and held it out.

Tom did not seem to see. Even when Indigo climbed up right beside him he did not look up. He did not move when Indigo bent down and wrapped the jacket around his shoulders.

The rain squall passed and turned to drizzle again. Behind them in the school, bells rang, footsteps hurried, doors opened and closed.

"I'm going back in for your coat and your stuff," said Indigo, when it began to look as if Tom meant to spend the afternoon hunched on the fire escape in the rain. "I'll be as quick as I can. Then we'll go home."

Tom did not move.

In the classroom an English lesson was now in progress. The teacher who was giving it had been told that Tom was sick and Indigo had gone out with him, and no further details.

"Is Tom feeling any better?" he asked as Indigo dashed into the classroom.

That was a question with too many answers for Indigo to begin to think of. He said, "He wants his jacket," and seized it from the back of a chair. A red rubber ball fell out of one of the jacket pockets, and he bent and scooped it up.

"Does he want that, too?" enquired the teacher, rather snidely, because he did not admire Tom's ball-bouncing skills.

"Yes."

"Is he being looked after?"

"Yes," said Indigo, thinking he himself was looking after Tom.

"Well, then, please sit down! You have wasted enough time. The lesson is nearly over. Tom can manage without his jacket for a few minutes longer, I'm sure."

"But I said I'd fetch it for him!"

"*Sit* please, Indigo! And take down the homework set on the blackboard. Then you can go."

Furious, Indigo sat down. Across the aisle from him the red-haired gang leader leaned over and murmured, "You want to be more careful, Casson! You could really hurt someone, pulling away a chair like that!"

Indigo swung angrily around to face him. From across the room the teacher called sharply, "What's going on over there?"

"Indigo's a little upset," explained the gang leader. "Because of Tom. Tom sat down and missed his chair and Indigo couldn't help laughing. . . ."

"Of all the stupid, dangerous tricks!" exclaimed the teacher. "Why did no one tell me before? Where is Tom now?"

"He's fine, sir," said the red-haired gang leader smoothly. "I saw him when I went out to fetch those books for you. Someone was with him." He glanced quickly at Indigo, as if to say, I am controlling this.

Out in the corridor a bell sounded.

"Get off for your next class everyone," ordered the teacher, glancing irritably around at the rabble's eager faces. "Indigo, stay here!"

The class melted discreetly away. Indigo said, "I didn't pull Tom's chair away!"

"Did anyone say you did?"

"I didn't laugh, either!"

"I should hope not. You know, Indigo, that this school does not tolerate bullying?"

"Yes, but . . ."

67

"Or fighting. Look at your hands."

Indigo realized then that his hands were raised, clench-knuckled, in the air. He lowered them slowly.

"That's better. Have you and Tom quarrelled?"

"No. Tom's my friend."

"I'm glad to hear it. Tell him I want to see him before the end of the day, please."

"Yes, sir," said Indigo, knowing that he had been away much too long and now only wanting to get away quickly.

The teacher nodded and hurried away to his next class. Indigo turned and ran down the corridor.

One glance through the door to the back playground showed him that Tom had gone.

"Lost your little friend, Casson?" asked the redhaired gang leader, shouldering by with a troop of rabble.

"Oh, leave me alone!" shouted Indigo.

"We do," said a passing voice. "That's what we do!" and then there was a wave of laughter.

Indigo waited until they had passed and then opened the door again. Tom was nowhere in sight, but the jacket he had lent to him was hanging across the chain that closed off the fire escape.

Indigo stepped outside and picked it up.

Tom had folded his jacket so that the inside was still dry. He could have thrown it in a wet angry heap, but he hadn't.

The rain that had fallen all day had stopped at last, and all at once, while Indigo stood there, the sun appeared.

Reflected light leaped upward from the puddled playground, dazzling Indigo's eyes. The unexpected brightness made him suddenly lighthearted. He put his jacket on and went to look for Tom.

Chapter Six

INDIGO SEARCHED EVERYWHERE, BUT HE WAS NOT able to find Tom in school that Friday afternoon. Eventually he gave up and caught the bus home with Saffron and Sarah. They all came into the kitchen together just as Rose was thumping down the telephone receiver.

"Who was that?" Saffron asked her.

"Stupid Daddy."

"Oh?"

"Asking about soup. He says I wrote him a letter all about soup. I didn't. I only put the soup in at the end. It wasn't the important part. Anyway, he's not coming home. So."

"Never mind, Rosy Pose," said Sarah consolingly.

"I don't mind! Good! That's what I say! Whose jacket is that, Indigo?"

"Tom's. He left it at school. I'm going to take it to his house for him."

"Can I come? Where does he live?"

"I know," said Sarah. "In the house with the yew trees next door to my old school. His grandmother talks to my mother sometimes. She's turned her house into a cattery. It's full of cats."

"If it's a cattery," observed Saffron, tipping a huge pile of weekend homework onto the kitchen table, "obviously it will be full of cats! What'll we start with? French, Spanish, math? Not IT. We'll do that on your computer, when we've taken Rose into town."

"I don't want to be taken into town," said Rose ungratefully. "I want to go with Indigo."

"Not now," said Saffron. "Tomorrow morning. To get your glasses checked. Sarah's mother says you ought to, and ours says you can."

"It'll be fun," said Sarah. "Anything might happen! But go with Indy now while Saffron and I get started on this lot. Come on, Saffy! Worst first! Math. Let's see if we can get it done before Indy and Rose come back. *If* they come back! I always used to be afraid of that house when I was little. I don't know why."

"It's spooky!" said Rose.

She stood on the pavement regarding Tom's

house while Indigo read aloud the notice by the gate.

THE YEWS

BOARDING CATTERY

Loving Care and Attention in Luxury Surroundings

VACCINATED CATS ONLY

"It's very spooky," said Rose, clutching the bundle that was Tom's jacket and school bag.

"It's just quiet," said Indigo, but secretly he agreed with Rose.

From the road all that could be seen were dark yew trees, with tall chimneys rising above them, but as Rose and Indigo set off down the weedy drive they caught glimpses of a garden as untidy as the Cassons' own.

"*And* it's full of cats," said Rose.

That was true. Their progress was watched by at least half a dozen pairs of greeny-gold eyes, blinking among the shadows. Halfway along they caught sight of a person moving across the grass near the back of the house.

"That must be Tom's grandmother," said Indigo. "We'd better go and say hello. Come on. Smile. Be polite. Hello, Mrs. Levin?"

"Yes. Can I help you?"

Rose, smiling and polite, remarked, "It's like a cat zoo here. Cats everywhere."

"And who might you be?" inquired Tom's grand-mother, looking intently from Indigo to Rose, and then back to Indigo again.

"I'm Indigo Casson," he explained, laying a hush-ing hand on Rose's shoulder. "Tom's in my class at school. We've brought some things he left behind this afternoon. This is my little sister, Rose."

"Little sister?" repeated Tom's grandmother, look-ing again at Rose. "How very interesting! I must tell Tom!"

"Is he in?"

"I couldn't say," said his grandmother, rather impatiently. "He comes and goes as he pleases. No sense of responsibility . . . just like his mother . . . Has he told you about his mother?"

"Bears?" asked Rose hopefully.

"Bears!" said Tom's grandmother scornfully. "I ask you! At her age! I really do not know what to make of her. . . ."

"Don't you like bears?" asked Rose, wriggling under Indigo's hand.

"Of course I like bears," said Mrs. Levin, looking at Rose as if something amused her. "But not to the exclusion of all else! Now, I'm afraid I must get on. I must see to the cats. The side door of the house is not locked. Open it and call Tom if you like."

She gave them a little nod of dismissal and then headed off in the direction of a row of cinder block and wire enclosures at the back of the house.

"She's a witch," said Rose, much too soon.

"Rose!"

"Poor Tom!"

"What if she had heard you?" demanded Indigo.

"Then she'll know I know. Listen! Listen a minute!"

Indigo, who was steering Rose firmly away from the back of the house, paused for a moment.

"Music!" said Rose.

It seemed to be coming from high above them, a phrase of melody with chords underneath, repeated, then stopped, then repeated again, carefully, several times.

"Somebody's playing something," whispered Rose.

Single notes sounded, very fast like a shower of stars.

"They are playing in patterns!" said Rose, entranced. "The notes are in patterns!"

Then the melody came again, stronger and clearer.

"I think it's a guitar," said Indigo. "It must be Tom."

As quietly as they could, he and Rose made their way to the side door of the house.

"I'll open it," whispered Rose.

The music paused at the opening of the door, then continued once more, but now very slowly, one note at a time, as if the player was listening intently.

"Tom!" called Indigo.

The playing stopped in a moment, and silence fell on them like a slab from the sky.

From the garden behind, Tom's grandmother called, "Tom's room is at the top of the stairs, if you want to go up."

"Thank you," Indigo called back, but he grabbed Rose and said, "No, Rose! Don't go up!"

"Why not? She said we could!"

"He knows we are here. He'd come down if he wanted to see us."

"But I've got his jacket and his bag for him! Let me go. I'll knock. I won't just go in."

Before Indigo could stop her she had pulled away,

hurried up the stairs, and was knocking on the door of the room at the top. It swung open at her touch, and there was Tom's room, bare and tidy and empty. No Tom, no guitar, nothing but the wind blowing through the open window.

"Leave his things and come down right now!" ordered Indigo, and he began walking away before she could begin to argue.

Rose did as she was told. As he reached the end of the drive he heard her come running up behind him.

"Don't be mad," she said. "I only wanted to see him."

"I know."

"I wonder where he is."

As if in answer, a few notes floated down from the sky.

Indigo put his finger to his lips to warn Rose to be silent, and turned back to scrutinize the old gray house behind its screen of trees. After a minute he found what he was looking for and motioned to Rose to come and see.

Rose followed the direction of his pointing finger with her eyes but could make out nothing unusual.

"He's right up there," murmured Indigo. "On

that little flat roof over the front door . . . Listen!"

The drifting notes were coming together to become the intricate background to a melody.

"He's humming!" whispered Rose. "Playing his guitar and humming on the roof. Isn't he?"

Indigo nodded.

They listened together until the melody stopped, and the guitar trailed away into quietness.

"Home, Rosy Pose!" said Indigo at last, turning away. "We've been ages!"

"I *love* people who play guitars on roofs!" said Rose, hopping along the pavement in one of her sudden happy moods. "Don't you?"

"Never knew anyone else who did it!"

"Don't you like Tom?"

"Of course I do. But I don't know about all the other guitar-on-roof players! They might be really awful people, with just that one good thing about them. Playing guitars on roofs . . . Or bagpipes . . . Or drums . . . Sarah would like that, and Saffy could have the bagpipes! Caddy could have a harp. . . . What about Mum?"

"One of those gourds filled with beans!" said Rose at once. "And Daddy could have a grand piano. On a flat roof. With a balcony and pink flowers in pots around the edge! And I'll have a very loud trumpet! What about you?"

"I'll just listen," said Indigo.

The following morning Rose went into town with Saffron and Sarah. Sarah, whose legs would only hold her up for very short distances, was in her wheelchair. Today she was in one of her wild moods where she bowled along at a terrible pace with cries of "Push faster!" The journey into town became a mad scurry, with breathless pauses during which they had to extract the wheelchair from the various obstacles into which it had been accidentally steered. Rose enjoyed it all very much.

However, once they reached the main shopping area, it was a different matter. Saffron and Sarah were dedicated shoppers. All their favorite shops had to be checked, and any new stock subjected to their detailed and critical scrutiny. Progress grew slower and slower. By the time they reached the department store that held the optician's office, Rose was completely bored.

Rose's glasses and eyes were checked again, and

she was told they were the exact prescription she needed, nothing wrong with them in any way.

"But she said she couldn't see anything through them!" protested Saffron.

"I didn't," said Rose. "I said I could see too much. Anyway, I don't want to change them. They work all right in the dark."

"You will get used to them in time," said the optician kindly, and turned away to talk to Sarah, who was going through a display of Italian sunglasses, just in case summer should ever come again.

Rose wandered over to the window, and while she was there she heard Saffron remark casually to Sarah, "There's Indigo's Tom," and nod at a boy crossing the road just in front of the store.

"Mmmm," said Sarah. "Look at these. Red lacquer. Too red?"

"Not sure. Let me try them."

"*Much* too red. Try those ones with tiny gold specks. . . ."

Rose slid toward the door. Saffron and Sarah, completely absorbed in designer labels, took no notice at all.

Rose slipped out of the store. Then she dodged

across the crowded pavement, glanced behind her to check she had not been followed, and sprinted in front of six lanes of Saturday-morning traffic.

Cars braked, horns blared, people shouted, and a bus driver swerved and swore. On the far pavement Tom turned to see what all the commotion was about. He was just in time to catch Rose as she landed triumphantly on the curb in front of him.

From high up on some nearby scaffolding a small group of workmen broke into applause.

Tom looked up at them with a quick, unwilling grin. Rose took no notice at all, but beamed at Tom and announced, "I wanted to see you!"

"Certainly seems like you did!" agreed Tom, looking meaningfully into the road where the traffic was just beginning to untangle itself again. "Do you usually cross the street that way?"

"I was in a hurry."

"There must be someone around here who's supposed to be in charge of you?"

"I don't need anyone to be in charge of me!" said Rose scornfully.

"I bet you've escaped from your mother!"

"I haven't. She's at home."

"She know you're in town?"

"'Course she does."

Tom gave up. Clearly Rose had a very careless family somewhere, but that was not his problem. He began to head off down the street again. Rose hopped cheerfully along beside him.

"Where are you going?" she asked.

"Music shop around the corner."

"To buy something?"

"Just to look."

"All right," said Rose.

At the music shop Tom stopped again.

"You still here, whoever you are?"

"I'm Rose," said Rose, sounding very surprised that he did not know this. "Indigo's my brother."

"Ohhhh," said Tom, beginning to understand.

"We came to your house last night. We brought your jacket and your school bag."

"Yes. Thanks."

"And we heard you playing. On that little high-up roof over the front door." Rose moved past Tom to gaze into the shop window, which was full of guitars propped up on stands. "Which one of these is like yours?"

"None of them."

"We saw your grandmother."

"She's a witch," said Tom absentmindedly, peering into the shadows at the back of the shop.

"I could tell. Cats too."

"Yep, cats too."

"It sounded lovely, your guitar. . . ."

"It's a useless guitar," said Tom, suddenly gloomy. "It's about as bad as they get. That's the one I want. Hanging on the wall, right at the back. See?"

"That black one?"

"That's the one. I came and tried it out twice last week. I was afraid they'd have sold it by now."

Rose nodded, and it seemed to Tom that she at least partly understood how bad that would be. He pushed open the shop door, and she followed him in as if trying out guitars was part of her usual Saturday morning routine.

A man behind a counter recognized Tom and came forward to meet them, smiling and asking, "Same as before?"

"Yes please," said Tom.

The black guitar was lifted down and handed to him. Tom found one of the empty stools kept for people who wanted to try out instruments, and began to play.

Nobody took any notice at all of Rose.

Rose did not mind that. She found another stool and sat down in a corner to listen as the back of the shop was filled with chords and melodies and humming notes. Already she knew why Tom wanted the black guitar. Even Rose could tell that the sounds she was hearing were far brighter and stronger than the ones of the night before.

It was a long time, at least half an hour, before the assistant returned and silently held out his hand.

"I did you a favor a minute ago," he said. "I just turned a customer away. Told him I thought it was sold."

"Thank you." Tom slowly eased himself up from his stool and undid the strap across his shoulders.

"It's too good a bargain to stay here long. If you could get a deposit together we could put it away for you."

Tom shook his head. "I would if I could."

"Well, maybe you'll think of a way," said the assistant, and he looked almost as regretful as Tom as he hung the black guitar back in its place on the wall. "Next time don't make it sound so good!"

Tom grinned and went over to the counter, where he chose a couple of plastic picks out of a box by the till. The assistant shook his head at the pound coin he offered for them and said they were on the house.

"You sure?" asked Tom.

"Yes. No problem. You come in again if you like."

"Thank you."

"How much is that black guitar?" asked Rose, speaking for the first time in ages.

"Four hundred and fifty pounds," the salesman told her.

"Oh."

"Should be a lot more, only we don't have the turnover here. It would be well over a thousand new."

Rose did not say any more, but outside in the street she paused to look at the display in the window again and asked, "Wouldn't one of those do instead?"

"No," said Tom.

Rose sighed. "Oh well. What shall we do now?"

"I don't know," said Tom, raising his eyebrows a little at the "we." He looked around and then up at the sky, which was a pale cold blue and full of scudding clouds. "This town is so *flat,*" he said irritably. "Let's get up somewhere a bit high."

• • •

Saffron and Sarah, panicking more every minute, searched the department store. Then the shops along the street outside. Then the marketplace. Every few minutes Sarah got out her mobile phone and rang Saffron's home. Nobody answered. Indigo was in the garden, cleaning out the guinea pig hutch that Caddy had reluctantly left behind when she went to university. Eve was in the shed, blocking in the background of a painting with the help of a wallpaper sample, because the buyer had requested a picture that would blend in with mint green stripes. She was very glad Bill was not coming home that weekend. She could imagine his comments all too easily. Not exactly art.

Bill himself was at a London exhibition. ["Pre-opening drinks, darling," he had explained (not to Eve). "May meet someone useful." "Off you go then, darling," said Darling.]

Caddy was in London, too, rallying for peace with another temporary boyfriend ("Perfectly Harmless Patrick. Mum might like him"). Peace rallying was a slow business, so Caddy whiled away the boring bits by composing in her head another letter to Michael (Darling, darling Michael . . .).

Michael also could be accounted for. He was taking a first-aid course which he knew would be useful one day, perhaps when Caddy, whose future was entwined with his, achieved her ambition of employment on a big game reserve, somewhere hot.

Even Derek-from-the-camp was where he ought to be, lying half in and half out of his sleeping bag, doodling a picture in the margin of his thesis (*Physics and the Paranormal*). It could have been Caddy, or it could have been Eve. He was no good at art.

Only Rose was where she should not be.

Saffron and Sarah searched the town's two art shops. The fancy one that Bill patronized when forced to buy stock out of London ("You expect to have to pay if you want quality"), and the scruffy one (which also sold birthday cards, fireworks, and unbelievably cheap watches) where Eve always went because they gave fantastic discounts on squashed tubes of paint.

Rose was in neither of these places.

Rose was with Tom. They were standing on top of the concrete box that covered the ventilation shaft on the highest level of the multistory car park. No one was about. Nobody ever parked up there, except in the weeks before Christmas.

Rose felt quite safe. If she fell it would only be the few feet to the car park below. She was telling Tom how frightened Indigo used to be of heights, and how he had almost, but not quite, cured himself by rappelling out of his bedroom window.

From so high up Rose and Tom could look right down into the marketplace. It looked beautifully organized. The people (little moving blurs of color to Rose) seemed unhesitatingly to follow predestined routes among the stalls. Tom pointed out the skateboarders, who he said he was controlling with his Programmable Invisible Remote Control Skateboard Handset. Everyone had programmable skateboards in America, he explained to Rose, and they were very useful. Mothers and fathers put their little kids on them, programmed in the coordinates, and sent them round the park for hours on end, perfectly safe. Rose listened happily, laughing in the right places and not interrupting too often. Tom found himself liking her more and more. It was a long time since he had had such an uncritical audience.

It was late in the afternoon before Rose got home. Even so she beat Saffron and Sarah, who in desperation had gone to the police station. By then they had managed to lose not only Rose, but also Sarah's mobile phone. However a policewoman telephoned home for them, and Eve, who was out of her shed by then, answered at once and said, "But Rose is here. With me. She came in a few minutes ago. She found her way home all by herself. She's drawing . . . what are you drawing, Rose darling?"

"Tom on the roof," said Rose.

"Drawing Tom on the roof," related Eve, being as helpful as possible because after all she was dealing with the police. "With pastels. Not oil based."

"I am using *some* oil based," said Rose. "For the highlights."

"*Some* oil based," said Eve contritely, and would have prattled on in this way for hours and hours if the policewoman hadn't tactfully shut her up.

Indigo, who had heard Rose's account of her afternoon, came to look at her picture.

"Did you like Tom then, Rose?" he asked.

"Yes," said Rose.

Chapter Seven

EVE SAID, "I REALLY NEED A FEW MORE POWER POINTS IN my shed," and she bought a very long extension cord with three sockets on the end. She plugged one end in at the wobbly switch that was shared by the washing machine, and then she led the cable out through the kitchen window, and all the way down the garden path to her shed, cleverly twisting it round the washing line posts to keep it off the ground.

"Fancy me being good at DIY!" she said happily to the watching guinea pigs in their hutch at the end of the garden.

The other end of the cable went in at the shed window. There Eve triumphantly installed an electric heater, a kettle, and the fiber optic lamp that the young offenders, to whom she taught art, had bought for her at Christmas.

"Luxury," said Eve, switching everything on.

The kettle boiled over and flooded the heater, blue

flames shot out of the wobbly plug by the washing machine, and all the lights went out. Rose wrote another scary letter to her father.

Darling Daddy,

This is Rose.

So flames went all up the kitchen wall. Saffron called the fire brigade and the police came too to see if it was a trick and the police woman said to Saffron Here You Are Again because of when I got lost having my glasses checked. But I was with Tom whose grandmother is a witch on top of the highest place in town.

Love, Rose.

It took Rose a long time, but she knew it would be worth the effort. It left her father with no alternative but to rush home and check out the state of the kitchen wall, the police records on missing children, Tom's grandmother, and the safety of the highest place in town. She awaited her father's next communication with great eagerness, pouncing on every telephone call, until the right one finally came.

"Now then, Rose!" said her father briskly. "I've

got your letter! What is all this about needing to have your glasses checked?"

Rose, who was a great basher-down of telephone receivers, bashed it down again.

The second week of term began, and for Indigo and Tom it was as bad as the first. One morning four windows in the language corridor were found to be broken, and a ball, very like the sort that Tom carried about, was discovered at the scene of the crime.

Tom was called into the Head's office and asked a lot of questions, not all of them about the windows.

Was Tom unhappy? the Head asked. Was there anything that he would like to talk about? Tom was visiting England, the Head understood, at his own request. Did he not want to make a success of the experience? Had he, for instance, made any particular friends?

Tom, except for remarking in a couldn't-care-less kind of way that he knew nothing about the smashed windows, took no notice of any of this. He gazed at the Head, bored and expressionless, looking like someone idly waiting for the rain to stop.

In his pocket was a note from Rose, delivered by Indigo the day before.

Dear Tom,

It is still there. My class was doing a
traffic survey in the marketplace so I went
around the corner and looked and it is still there.

Love, Rose.

In all the time that Tom had been in England he had
not sent a message to anyone. Not to his friends at
home, nor his mother (toiling away among the bears
in Yellowstone National Park), or even to the father
he talked so much about.

But he had replied to Rose:

THANK YOU. I AM GOING TO HAVE
ANOTHER LOOK AT IT ON SATURDAY.

TOM.

Indigo had delivered both messages without any
fuss.

It was beginning to dawn on Tom that Indigo was
not quite the fool he had seemed at first. That was
partly why he had bothered to take any notice of Rose,
because she was Indigo's younger sister. In Tom's opinion, younger sisters were among the worst of family

calamities. On Saturday, when he had realized who Rose was, he had slowed down to take a look at her in the same awful-but-fascinated way that people slow down to look at traffic accidents. Expecting the worst.

His fingers touched her note in his pocket. He guessed that it might not have been easy for her to sneak away from the traffic survey to visit the music shop. It made him smile to think of her doing it. He had kept her note, like he would have kept a message from any friend.

"Are you *listening* to me, Tom?" demanded the Head sharply.

Tom jerked his thoughts away from Rose and Indigo and the black guitar, and was beginning to treat the Head to one of his most insolent, slow-motion shrugs when there came a knock at the office door.

"Wait outside please!" called the Head, and then, "I *said* WAIT OUTSIDE!" as the door opened.

To Tom's enormous surprise, Indigo appeared.

Indigo said, without any apology or introduction, "Tom didn't break those windows. Think about it! How's Tom going to throw his ball through a window and then get it back again to throw through the next? Four times? How would he get it back each time? And why would he leave it there afterward to get himself into trouble? It would have taken two people to smash those windows, one to throw the ball through, and the other to throw it back again. And they'd need people keeping guard while they did it."

The Head popped his eyes out at Indigo in the unpleasant way he had, and said, "Thank you, Indigo! My powers of reasoning had actually led me thus far!"

"Why are you yelling at Tom, then?" asked Indigo.

"*Out* you go, Indigo!" snapped the Head. "*Out! Now!* That's right! And you, Tom! I see you seem to have made one friend at least. *Off* you go, both of you!"

To Indigo's surprise he was suddenly sounding quite human. Also, he had clearly had enough of them. He herded them out of his room so fast that they nearly fell over the large clump of rabble who were listening at the door.

"Ah!" said the Head, popping out his eyes again.

Tom took a ball out of his pocket right under the Head's nose.

Nothing happened.

Tom bounced it.

The Head looked away.

The rabble muttered indignantly.

Tom raised his eyebrows maliciously at them, said, "Come on, Indigo!" and set off down the corridor, bouncing his ball.

The Head still seemed not to notice, so Marcus, a particularly slow-thinking rabble member, unwisely pointed it out, saying, "Look, sir! That's how those windows got smashed!"

"Is it really, Marcus?" said the Head, menacingly. "I think in the future you would be sensible to keep your opinions to yourself!"

Marcus's friends thought so too. They cornered him in gang headquarters during afternoon break and told him so.

"You don't do *anything* that I don't tell you to do," ordered the red-haired leader. "And you keep your mouth shut until *I* tell you to speak!"

"I don't see why," said Marcus, so they explained why.

"*Now* do you understand?" demanded the red-haired leader, panting a little. Marcus was heavy, and the explaining had required so much muscle, he had been forced to lend a hand.

"Yes," muttered Marcus, very flushed and damp and unhappy.

"Yes, *thank you*," prompted the leader gently.

"Yes, thank you," said Marcus, but obviously he did not really understand, because the next day at soccer training he tackled Tom so viciously and so publicly he was sent off the field.

Later on he had to endure another explanation.

Afterward Marcus went home and feigned an illness so well that his worried mother let him stay away from school the next day. Josh, his best friend, who had been very frightened and didn't understand why Marcus had not drowned, fell victim to the same illness. He was allowed to stay at home too.

After a day or two, however, they both had to go back, and although they were relieved to discover the incident appeared to have been forgotten, their happy rabble days were over. Their hearts were not in it anymore. They could not forget that Marcus had only been released the second time because Tom himself had intervened.

Tom had heard the grunts and splashes of the toilet-dunking explanations and set about kicking down the cubicle door with indiscreet yells of, "Stop it, or I'll kill you!"

Part of the rabble had to be redeployed to shut

him up, and then Indigo Casson suddenly appeared and joined in the attack. They made so much noise between them that Marcus had been reluctantly hauled back to dry land.

"You wait, Levin!" snarled the red-haired gang leader, afterward. "And you, Casson!"

Despite their apparent victory, the skin on the back of Indigo's neck prickled with fear. The red-haired gang leader saw it in his eyes and laughed.

Tom looked from one to the other, heaved a big sigh, said, "Catch!" and threw his ball to Indigo. Indigo missed and the ball went rolling away along the corridor.

"Useless," said Tom, jogging off to retrieve it. "Try again! Gosh, how could you miss that? Didn't your father ever teach you to catch a ball?"

"No," said Indigo, grinning at the thought of Bill doing such a thing. "He's not a baseball player! He paints things."

"Houses?"

"Pictures. Art. He's an artist in London. We don't see him much."

Tom gave him one of his quick, considering glances and asked, "Doesn't he live with you?"

"No," said Indigo, finally saying out loud what he had known now for a long, long time. "Not really. Not anymore."

"Do you mind?"

"It happened so slowly," said Indigo, "I suppose I got used to it without noticing too much. Rose minds. And she's only eight. She worries about things. Don't tell her what happened just now."

"I don't suppose I'll see her again," said Tom.

Indigo grinned. Since Saturday, Rose had put in a good deal of work on the picture on the kitchen wall. Sarah, who had previously occupied a prime spot on one side of the chimney, had been ruthlessly swept away. She had reappeared some time later, talking to Saffron, farther along the roof. A shadowy outline now lounged in Sarah's place, holding a guitar.

"I think you probably will see Rose again," said Indigo to Tom.

Caddy came home on Friday evening. Perfectly Harmless Patrick brought her in his battered old car.

"Patrick's the one with the chinchilla," said Caddy, by way of introduction.

Perfectly Harmless Patrick said, "Hi! Hi! Gorgeous!"

and fell asleep on the sofa holding a full mug of coffee.

"Crikey, Caddy!" said Indigo, and disappeared upstairs to tell Rose.

Eve murmured, "Sweet," rather doubtfully.

Sarah said, not doubtfully at all, "Horrendous! The worst yet. Rock bottom."

"He had a very difficult childhood," said Caddy as she removed the mug of coffee from his unresisting fingers.

"Who didn't?" asked Saffron unsympathetically. "Gosh, he's ancient, Caddy! Look, he's going bald! All that long trailing stuff is just a disguise!"

"If I was going bald," said Sarah, "I would face the fact and have it all shaved off."

"Well, I thought Mummy might like him," said Caddy defensively. "He's sensitive, that's what he told me. He says he needs mothering. Anyway, I can always take him back."

"I think you're going to have to, Caddy darling," said Eve. "Even if he didn't need mothering (which after all is only another way of saying he needs a slave), sensitive people are so terribly . . ."

"Sensitive," said Saffron.

"Well," said Eve, "they are generally quite useless

at practical things. Like sorting out the wiring . . . Anyway, I must get on with some work. Cats to paint! Hello, Rose darling! Come in and see what Caddy has brought home to show us!"

She escaped, and Rose, who had already heard the news from Indigo, glanced at Patrick and began laughing.

"See?" said Sarah. "Rose knows! *Absolutely* rock bottom! You *cannot* be serious, Caddy!"

"Oh, stop looking at him!" said Caddy, uncomfortably. "I'll find something to cover him up with in a minute!"

"How long are you leaving him there for?" asked Rose.

"Just until Sunday," said Caddy, trying to sound casual.

"Till Sunday!" repeated Saffron. "So is Michael dumped?"

"Of course he isn't!" said Caddy indignantly. "I've never dumped anyone!"

"Start!" said Saffron. "Otherwise they just pile up, taking up the sofas. . . . Come on! Do this one right now!"

"I'll do him later," said Caddy, and slid out of the

room, followed by Rose, who wanted to show her the latest developments on the kitchen wall. Saffron and Sarah were left alone with Patrick, who had begun to snore.

"Sunday!" groaned Saffron, looking at him. "*Sunday!* I can't believe it!"

Her voice must have penetrated Patrick's sleeping mind because he woke up all at once and moaned blearily, "Sunday! *Sunday!* Wha . . . timisit?"

"Nearly seven o'clock," Sarah told him.

"At night?"

"Yep!"

"Nearl' sevna' clock!" repeated Patrick, clutching his head and rocking backward and forward. "And Sunday! Igottagetbackon Sunday! Howlongavabin asleep?"

"What?"

"Howlong ava bin asleep?"

"Oh!" said Saffron, suddenly diabolically inspired with a means of getting rid of him. "Gosh, ages! Fast asleep since Friday!"

"We thought you'd never wake up," said Sarah.

"Well . . . Igotta . . . begoin!" said Patrick, and began a sort of slow-motion panic, hitting himself in a clumsy, sleepy kind of way, groaning, "Carkeys! Carkeys!"

Sarah and Saffron looked at each other, baffled for a moment, and then Sarah understood and said, "He wants his car keys! There they are! On the floor beside him!"

"What! Oh right! Car keys! There you are Patrick!"

"Carkeys," said Patrick, grabbing them. "Savedmilife!" And heaving himself off the sofa, he staggered into the kitchen, shaking his head as if to test how firmly it was still attached. "Caddy . . . Caddy! Gotta go! Bigrushon!"

"What, right now?" asked Caddy, very surprised. "I can't possibly!"

"Well I gotta . . . Where . . . dileave . . . acar?"

"I'll show you," said Saffron, steering him firmly out of the door and hissing over her shoulder, "Shut *up,* Caddy! Say *nothing*! . . . Come on, Patrick, this way!"

She closed the kitchen door securely behind herself as she followed him out and led him to his car.

"Carkeys! Carkeys!" moaned Patrick.

"In your hand," said Saffron, taking them from him and unlocking the door.

"Binalovely . . . break."

"Fantastic," agreed Saffron, pushing him gently in. "Car keys! That's right! Put your lights on, I should. Soon be dark! Don't worry about Caddy, we'll look after her."

"Peacedarlin," said Patrick gratefully.

"Perfect," said Saffron. "Off you go then!"

She spent a moment waving good-bye before rushing back indoors and calling urgently, "Turn the lights off! Turn all the house lights off so he won't have anywhere to head back for if he suddenly wakes up!"

"But I don't understand!" protested Caddy. "He was staying until *Sunday*!"

"He did," said Saffron. "At least, he thinks he did. Now let's everyone lie down on the floor so it looks like nobody's in! Go on, Rose! And you, Sarah! How *could* you have thought he would do for Mum, Caddy?"

"What do you mean?" asked Rose. "Why would Mummy want him? What for?"

"Nothing," said Caddy soothingly. "He was mine. My mistake. It was his chinchilla I really fell for. Never mind, he's gone now."

Rose asked no more questions, but late that night

she switched on her bedside light and wrote another letter.

Darling Daddy,

This is Rose.

The shed needs new wires now it has blown up.

Caddy is bringing home rock-bottom boyfriends to see if they will do for Mummy.

Instead of you.

Love, Rose.

Chapter Eight

ON SATURDAY MORNING ROSE WAS UP AND ABOUT VERY early, making lots of noise. Indigo woke and heard her, thumping and banging, down in the empty kitchen, complaining, "I've lost my shoes! I've lost my shoes!"

The shoe hunting noises got louder and then stopped. Rose came marching crossly up the stairs, intent on getting her family out of bed to help.

"Saffron, I know you are awake!"

Saffron groaned and pulled her quilt over her head.

"My shoes have disappeared!"

"Go 'way! Ask Caddy."

"Caddy's asleep."

"*I* was asleep!"

"Caddy, have you seen my shoes?"

"Shush, darling," murmured Caddy, deep in dreams.

Rose pulled open the curtains and removed the pillow Caddy had dragged over her head.

"What *is* the matter?" Caddy moaned. "Don't tell me Patrick has come back!"

"My shoes are gone."

"Glasses?" suggested Caddy dozily. "Perhaps if you had your glasses on? Yes? No?"

Rose stamped out of the room and returned to Saffron.

"Aren't you getting up yet? I need to go into town."

"Not with me! Never again! Ask Mum."

Eve was awake, blinking dopily in the middle of the big bed. Rose, who was used to finding her mother curled up very neatly on her own side, dutifully leaving space for an invisible Bill, noticed this but made no comment. Instead, she flopped down grumpily across Eve's legs.

"Ouch!" said Eve.

"How can I go into town without my shoes?"

Eve struggled out from under Rose and said, "Rose darling, if you go into town somebody will have to take you. And I don't think anybody is ready quite yet, darling."

"I'll go by myself, then. But I need my shoes."

"No, no, no, no, no!"

"No?" repeated Rose, astonished, because Eve hardly ever said no to anyone.

"I'm sorry, Rose! You can't go into town by yourself, and I can't take you. I'm giving my special art class down at the college. Have you seen the new posters?"

Rose's mother pointed to the bedroom mirror, which had a large bright poster taped onto the glass.

PAINT THE DREAM!
POSITIVE GRAFFITI!
SATURDAYS 10:30-12:00

"I thought you would like to come too. It'll be fun. Lovely students (court referrals mostly). Caddy will be there, she wants to meet them. And I could take you into town afterward."

"Afterward will be too late," said Rose discontentedly, and she slid off the bed and padded into Indigo's room.

Indigo had got himself up without Rose's help, rummaged through the upside-down kitchen, and discovered the missing shoes behind the rubbish bin.

Rose smiled for the first time that morning and asked hopefully, "Would you mind getting dressed and coming into town really quick, Indy? I have to go to Tom's black guitar shop, and I don't know what time it opens. I'm meeting him there."

"Does he know?" asked Indigo, very surprised.

"Yes. He said about it in that note you brought me. But he only said Saturday morning. He didn't say a time."

Indigo still looked very doubtful.

"Please, Indy."

"Could you have made a mistake?"

"I never make mistakes," said Rose, impatiently. "You know I don't! Hurry up and I'll make you a sandwich while you are getting ready!"

"Oh, all right," said Indigo.

Tom's grandmother said at breakfast time, "Please put that ball away before you knock something over! Shall you be around to help me this morning?"

"I helped last night!" protested Tom. "I cleaned out all those smelly runs!"

Tom's grandmother then delivered her "Most Boys Your Age Would Jump At The Chance To Work With Animals" speech, and while she tidied up the kitchen around him, followed it up with the one that began "Most Boys Your Age Are Expected To Help Far More Than You Are Ever Asked To."

Tom scooped up cereal and showed no sign of interest, waiting for the next paragraph ("I Can See Your Father And Mother Have Spoiled You. That Is The Trouble With Separated Parents. They Compete And The Child Ends Up Ruined . . ."). Anticipating the next line, he mouthed silently, "Or Is It Being Brought Up In America?" with his eyes on the ceiling.

"Or Is It Being Brought Up In America?" said his grandmother. "I *wish* you wouldn't shrug like that! Tom!"

"You Haven't Been Listening To A Word I've Said," recited Tom in his best British accent, and his grandmother suddenly smiled.

"Have you been climbing on the roof again? One of my customers thought she saw you up there last night. What will I say to your father if you fall and break your neck?"

"Tell him 'Good news. All your dreams have come true.'"

His grandmother sighed. "Have you something special you want to do this morning?"

"Yes," said Tom, taking his mug and cereal bowl across to the dishwasher.

"Not in there! It's full of cat dishes. Wash them at the sink. What happened to that friend of yours?"

"What friend?"

"He came here with his little sister. I liked him very much. Very nice to see a big boy taking care of his sister like that."

Tom's mug slipped through his fingers and landed in his cereal bowl, smashing them both.

"Sorry!" he said sullenly.

"Oh, really, Tom! All right, I can see it was an accident! Never mind. What was it you were planning to do this morning?"

"I just wanted to go to the music shop."

"I did ask you to put that ball away! Off you go, then, if you must. Don't forget to be back for lunch. . . . Oh look! Wait, Tom!"

She had followed him to the door, and discovered the mail on the doormat.

"One for you, from home . . ."

"I'll read it later," said Tom hurriedly, and fled up the drive and on to the long road into town.

There was a part of Tom that wished that he had never, in his awful self-imposed homesickness, wandered into the marketplace and discovered the music shop and the black guitar. It was one more complication in his already far-too-complicated life.

He began to calculate how many years he would need to go back to find his previous contented existence. He thought back a year at a time in his head.

This time last year?

That was awful, thought Tom firmly.

This time two years ago?

No.

Three years then?

That would make him nine years old. Tom decided he would be quite pleased to time travel back to nine years old. That year had been a good time. He had spent the summer with his mother, and when he came home again at the end, he had brought with him the old guitar. The following winter he had begun taking music lessons after school. By the time he was ten years old he was coming along well.

Then followed the two years that had really turned him into a player.

When Tom was ten years old he took to disappearing antisocially up to his bedroom the moment he came home from anywhere.

Once he overheard a conversation.

"Where's Tom?"

His father had replied, in an I-am-at-the-end-of-my-patience kind of voice, "Hiding upstairs!"

"I'm not!" Tom yelled furiously (and untruthfully). "I'm practicing my guitar!"

"Sorry, Tom," they both called immediately, and they really had been sorry. They were always very respectful about his guitar. Louise had a theory that it mattered very much to Tom because it had been given to him by his mother.

In the years that followed it had become the perfect excuse.

"Tom, come and help us pick the color of the new car! Come on! Your choice!"

"I'm practicing!"

"Tom! It's Christmas Eve, for goodness' sake!"

"Leave me alone."

"Tom. *Look* who's come home at last! Please, Tom!"

"I'm practicing. Leave me alone."

All the while Tom's fingers had grown stronger and quicker. They had learned to move across the strings faster than Tom could think them into their places. At first he had worked so hard because if he sat in silence they said he was sulking, but later on he played because it had become part of himself to play.

The guitar that Tom brought back from his mother's was an old Spanish one. It drove him crazy. The only thing right about it was that it *was* a guitar. Everything else was wrong. The back had a split in it and the neck was warped. The bass notes rattled. The tuning pegs were so loose that it went out of tune, said Tom's father, every time Tom slammed a door.

That was less than the truth. Tom was a frequent door slammer, but he did not do it every few minutes. That was how often his guitar seemed to go out of tune. It was just about worn out.

"Tom," said his father, just before his twelfth birthday, with catalogs from a dozen guitar shops gathered on the table beside him, "Come and look at these.

Come and talk to us about what you would like."

"I would like to be a million miles away," said Tom.

This dismal English town was as close as Tom had been able to get to a million miles away.

Tom turned off the main road into the little street where the music shop was and to his surprise saw Indigo and Rose, heading toward him from the opposite direction.

Rose hurried to meet him at once. Indigo followed behind, grinning a little sheepishly, noticing that Tom's eyebrows had risen as far as they could go.

"Have you managed to get the four hundred and fifty pounds yet?" demanded Rose as she came running up.

"No," replied Tom, and his eyebrows did not get any lower.

"I'll check if it's still there," said Rose, and hurried off to squash her nose against the music shop window while Indigo said to Tom, "She said you wanted her to come."

"She did?"

"And someone had to come with her. I'll be in the library. Can you bring Rose across to meet me there when you've finished?"

"Me?"

"Well, yes," said Indigo. "Or else I'll have to come into the shop and wait. You won't want a lot of people hanging around listening."

A lot of people hanging round listening would have suited Tom perfectly, and his eyebrows went up even higher, but then Rose called, "I can see it!" and he passed his hand across his hair and suddenly relaxed.

"Yes, I'll bring her across," he agreed, and hurried to peer in at the window beside Rose. A moment later he exclaimed in horror, "It's gone!"

"No. It isn't," said Rose calmly. "They moved it. It's in the dark corner behind the counter now. I asked them to put it there."

"You did?"

"When we came to town with the school. I said couldn't they put it where it wouldn't show up so much."

Tom looked at her in astonishment. Rose said complacently, "It hardly shows at all."

"Well, *come* on, then!" said Tom, suddenly laughing, and he pushed open the shop door and Rose followed him inside.

Indigo stayed where he was and watched through the plate glass window. Rose pointed to the black guitar. A man came forward and handed it over to Tom. Tom took it eagerly, strapped it over his shoulder, and began testing the strings. He plucked them one by one, and two by two, holding down a single note at a time, listening, adjusting the tuning pegs, listening again. His face took on a sealed, inward look. Indigo recognized the expression, he had seen it over and over again on Rose's face when she was engrossed in some picture.

Tom finished his tuning, looked at Rose, said something, and began to play.

Indigo went across to the library and settled himself down with a book. He thought he would probably be there for quite a long time.

"Guess who I went to see last week," said Caddy to her mother as they drove to the college where Eve taught art to young offenders on Saturday mornings. "Daddy. I went to his studio."

"Goodness, Caddy!"

"I suddenly wanted to see it. I never have before."

"I haven't been myself for years and years and years," said Eve. "Did you tell him you were coming?"

"No. I just went. And I found it quite easily and I rang the bell and there he was. Looking just like he always looks. You know, brown and posh and cheerful."

Eve sighed a little.

"And he said, 'Caddy darling, what a gorgeous surprise! Come in! Come in!'"

The last time Eve had visited Bill's studio had been before Rose was born, but she still remembered very clearly how he had flung the door open and exclaimed, "Eve darling, what a gorgeous surprise!"

"So I went in," said Caddy, "and it was all very beautiful and bare and shining and he made tea for me and we had it out on that tiny balcony where he grows mint and herbs and things."

"Oh yes. I remember."

"He has a table that is covered in photographs. Some I'd never seen. One of Indigo when he came out of the hospital just before Christmas all thin and hollow-looking. And one of Saffy and Sarah in the garden. And a big one of Rose with her glasses on that he said he took in the shop when they were choosing frames. She's looking into a mirror and there's another mirror behind her so she's reflected and reflected backward and forward, getting smaller and smaller."

"That does sound clever. What else?"

"Nothing. He was just nice."

"Was he all by himself? No one else there?"

"Yes, all alone. Poor Dad."

Caddy looked sideways at her mother and caught her eye. They both laughed.

"Oh well," said Eve. "Never mind. Here we are!"

She turned into the college car park, looked around, and then swerved suddenly toward a group of waving students.

"Spike and Lisa and Matthew," she explained to Caddy. "They always save me a parking place. . . . Brace yourself now, Caddy!"

"Why?"

"Well, darling," said Eve, jumping out and beginning to unload cans of spray paint and huge rolls of cardboard into the arms of her students, "I suppose Daddy would say it's not exactly art. . . ."

The man in the music shop was clearly on Tom's side. He said, "I was thinking. Have you got a guitar you could trade in against the price of that one? I could arrange a part exchange. Would that help you?"

"No," said Tom. "My guitar . . . I've got this

old Spanish guitar . . . No. It wouldn't help. Sorry."

The shop man said unhappily, "You know what it's worth, that one. Four-fifty is a gift."

"Yes."

"We gave three-eighty for it. Polished it up. Lemon oil on the neck, new strap, new strings. There's an old case round the back we could let you have with it."

Tom spread his hands helplessly.

"Could you bring someone in to hear it? How about your mother? . . ."

Tom shook his head and began to walk toward the door.

"Tom's mother's in America," Rose told the kind assistant, "looking after the bears in Yellowstone National Park."

"Oh."

"And his father's an astronaut," Rose continued, "on his way to a star. And his grandmother's a witch. I've seen her."

"Well," said the assistant, clearly bemused at this information. "I don't know what to say. Perhaps it's just not meant to be."

"It is," said Rose.

"Thanks anyway," said Tom. "Come on, Rose."

He left the shop and walked away quickly, not looking back, but Rose, who had gone out with him, suddenly turned and dashed back in. The shop assistant had his back to her. He was hanging up the black guitar, not in the dark corner, but back in the place where Tom had first shown it to her.

"Not there!" hissed Rose, so ferociously that he nearly jumped out of his skin. "*Not* there! And *don't* sell it!"

Tom suddenly remembered his promise to take Rose to the library. He had never in his life escorted anyone anywhere, but he had seen it being done. Also, he knew how recklessly Rose treated traffic. So when she caught up with him again at the crossing point on the main road he grabbed her very firmly around the wrist and did not let go until they had reached the central island and were waiting for the second set of lights to turn green.

"Look what you've done!" said Rose, displaying the purple marks Tom's fingers had left on her arm.

Tom did not reply. He was looking across to the far side of the road, where the red-haired gang leader and two of his friends were doubled up with laughter, pointing at him and calling.

"Isn't she a bit young for you, Levin?"

"Your father fetch her back from some planet for you, Tom?"

The lights turned green and Tom seized Rose again and marched her across. The red-haired gang leader and his friends went on their way, still hooting and calling. Rose heard one of them say sneeringly, "That's Indigo Casson's sister."

"Are they the boys who put Indigo down a toilet?" she demanded.

"Probably," answered Tom, hauling her along the pavement to the library as quickly as he could.

"Why?" asked Rose.

"What?"

"Why?"

"Oh. Well. I think he annoyed them."

To Rose that almost sounded as if Tom accepted this as a good enough reason.

"You can't be disgusting to people just because they annoy you!" she exclaimed very crossly. "*Thousands* of people annoy me! *Millions* of people annoy *millions* of people all the time!"

"That's true," agreed Tom, thinking bitter thoughts of home.

"You have to put up with them," said Rose.

Tom did not say anything to that.

Chapter Nine

BILL CASSON WAS NOT THE LEAST BIT DISTURBED BY ROSE'S remarks concerning his probable replacement by one of Caddy's rock-bottom boyfriends. He laughed. He thought it was a joke. What did bother him was the thought that one of the boyfriends might attempt to rewire Eve's shed. Rose's letter seemed to suggest the two problems—the rewiring of the shed, and the rock-bottom boyfriends—were somehow connected.

Just in case they were, Bill telephoned to forbid it.

Rose, as usual, answered the phone.

"Darling Rose," said her father, his heart sinking to his artistic boots at the sound of Rose's unhelpful voice, "I'm ringing about your letter. . . ."

"I knew you would!" interrupted Rose smugly.

"You *were* joking about Caddy's ridiculous boyfriends?"

"No."

"I'd better talk to Mummy then!"

Rose seemed to lose interest and started humming, as if she was bored and about to walk away.

"Don't hum, Rose! Off you go and tell Mummy that I need to talk to her about the wiring to the shed. . . ."

"What!" cried Rose. "Not about the rock-bottom boyfriends coming here instead of you?"

"Just the wiring, darling. Off you pop."

"Too late!" said Rose, most put out. "Derek-from-the-camp, who Mummy calls Darling Derek, *Darling Derek* came and did it yesterday! He dug a trench right down the garden and put the wire in that. He threaded it through a hose pipe."

Bill groaned.

"It took all day and afterward Mum cooked him a special supper to celebrate. And then he went to the garage and bought pink lilies because he remembered those were her favorite. He's very fond of her. So."

Rose waited hopefully for her father to say no one ought to be fond of Eve to the extent of pink lilies, but he did not seem to mind at all, so she went on.

"And then *Darling Derek* fixed proper plugs on the wall in the shed, so of course Mummy is very pleased."

"She won't be pleased when the circuit overloads

and the house goes up in smoke! I wish this . . . this . . . Derek, is it?"

"Darling Derek."

"Whatever. I wish he'd consulted me first. I'd be much happier if he'd left things alone."

"So would I," agreed Rose. "I bet we hardly ever see Mum anymore. She used to come out to make coffee and get warmed up but now that she's got a kettle and a proper electric heater she doesn't need to. She rang up last night to say it was bedtime."

"From the shed?"

"Yes."

"Good grief! Can you fetch this Derek, Rose? I think I should speak to him."

"He's gone back to his camp. He's guarding a stone circle."

"Mummy then."

"She's gone with him. She's going to paint it."

"You should have told me Eve wasn't home, Rose!" exclaimed Bill. "Who is looking after you?"

"Caddy."

"Go and find her then, darling," said Bill, a little impatiently. "Say Daddy wants to know something important about the fuse box."

"What can be important about a fuse box?"

"Rose!" thundered Bill.

"Oh, all right," said Rose, and put down the receiver. Her father heard her voice calling, "Caddy, Caddy," and her footsteps running up the stairs.

A minute later she was back again. "Caddy's still asleep," she announced. "She wasn't in until very very late last night. She was out with Michael."

"Please," begged Bill. "Please Rose, let me speak to someone! Saffron or Indigo?"

"They're at Sarah's."

"Rose," said her father pathetically, "do *you* happen to know whether that shed extension is wired properly to the fuse box?"

"Of course it is," said Rose promptly. "Labelled and everything! Paradise!"

"I beg your pardon?"

"Derek made a pink label and wrote PARADISE on it," explained Rose. "Let's stop talking about boring wiring! Do you know what Caddy said?"

"Tell me!"

"She said she went to visit you and you were nice!"

"Of course I was nice!"

"Oh."

"How's school, Rose?"

"Same as always."

"What have you been learning?"

"Nothing."

"What have you been doing then?"

"My great big picture."

Bill did not ask, as Rose longed for him to ask, "What great big picture?"

"You'll see it when you come home," she said.

"Lovely!"

"You're not on it!"

"Oh well. How would you like *me* to paint a picture of *you*, Rose?"

"We were talking about *my* picture that *I'm* painting!" shouted Rose.

"Of course we were!" agreed her father. "And it sounds marvel—"

"You can't say that without even seeing it!"

"No, no I can't! You are absolutely right! Only I must go now, Rosy Pose! *Don't* bang the phone down this time! Love to everyone . . ."

For once he beat Rose to it, getting the phone down before she did, disappearing back into the silence of his unknown London world.

Rose stood in the middle of the kitchen and shouted, "I hate him! I hate him!" until Caddy came staggering sleepily down the stairs and asked, "Who?"

"Daddy!"

"No, you don't. Have you had breakfast?"

"I don't want breakfast!" growled Rose.

"Just let me have a shower and I'll come down and make pancakes."

"Real pancakes?"

"Of *course,* Rose darling," said Caddy. "I am not just a beautiful zoologist! Oh, and I brought you some silver for your picture. It's a stick of graphite, really, but it makes a lovely silvery color. It's on the mantel-piece somewhere. Have a hunt."

Caddy went upstairs again, leaving Rose feeling a little better. She hunted along the mantelpiece until she found the graphite, a stick of metallic silver, cool and smooth as water, perfect for her picture.

Earlier in the week Eve had moved the fridge to give Rose extra space, and since then her picture had grown and grown. Now Tom's father's rocket whizzed across the sky, heading for a galaxy of stars. Beyond the stormy waters that Rose had drawn lapping the walls of the house, a small island had emerged, a distant view of America, with clearly visible bears. The sketch of Tom was still unfinished.

"I can't get his hands right," explained Rose as she watched Caddy mix up pancake batter. "I wish he'd come here and let me draw him properly, like Derek-from-the-camp did."

"Get Indigo to ask him," suggested Caddy, and when Indigo came in a few minutes later, he said that he would try. He and Saffron were both very bouncy, and extremely pleased to find Caddy and Rose cooking pancakes.

"Exactly what I felt like eating," said Saffron, hunting out plates. "And good news, Rose! Sarah's mother has invited us all for Sunday lunch. Roast chicken and lemon pie."

"Roast chicken and lemon pie!" repeated Rose, and abandoned her job of sugaring and stacking pancakes to sketch into her picture a tiny outline of Sarah's mother, sailing in a small boat toward the storm-washed house.

"Delivering Sunday lunch," explained Rose.

On Monday morning Indigo went in search of Tom as soon as he arrived at school. After a very short while he found him in one of the upstairs classrooms, doing what he liked to do best, entertaining an audience.

Tom was giving a display of his ball-throwing skills, with the help of a lump of blue chalk and a volunteer rabble member. He had cleared a semicircular space of chairs and tables and placed his volunteer against the classroom wall. By the time Indigo arrived he was already halfway through, tracing the boy's outline on the white paint of the wall behind him with a series of spectacular ball shots.

"Don't move!" ordered Tom.

Wham!

The ball, just missing the spread-eagled figure, smacked into the wall with an explosion of blue dust. Tom caught it on the rebound and chalked it again.

"Don't move!"

Wham!

Each throw left a circle of dusty blue on the wall. There was one at the point of each hand and foot, and one at each side of the volunteer's hips and shoulders.

Wham!

Wham!

That was a bounce beside each ear, done in two swift movements.

"Don't move!" commanded Tom, and finished off the show with a last perfect shot that just skimmed the top of the boy's head.

He caught the ball with a flourish, and there was a spontaneous outburst of applause.

"Cool!" said David, the volunteer, and there was a buzz of enthusiastic agreement that turned to groans when Tom, high on success, remarked, "My mother can do it on horseback!"

Here we go again, thought Indigo, and wished that Tom would learn to stop when he was winning.

"She practice on the bears?" asked someone facetiously.

For that he got the ball smack in the middle of his stomach.

This did not deter another person from demanding, "Can't she do it blindfolded, Tom?"

"Blindfolded on horseback?" shouted another.

"That would be too easy," drawled the red-haired gang leader. "Rides rodeo, doesn't she, Levin?"

"You keep your mouth shut!" snapped Tom.

"Come on, Tom!" urged Indigo, trying to divert Tom's attention before things got any worse. "Throw me that ball!"

But Tom was past the point when he could be diverted. A bell rang, and the class streamed out and along the upstairs corridor, still gibing at him.

"Throw Indigo the ball, Tom, before his big sister comes and gets you!"

"How many horses you got then, Tom? Just the one?"

The rabble were racing ahead now, enjoying themselves, galloping and neighing on pretend horses, heading for the first of the pair of staircases that led down to the main entrance hall of the school.

"Are you the biggest liar in America, Tom?" asked the red-haired gang leader pleasantly. "Or are they all like you over there?"

He was foolish enough to ask this question at the top of the stairs, turning back to smile into Tom's angry face.

Tom did the obvious thing. He gave the red-haired gang leader a huge and satisfying shove in the chest. Then, immediately cheerful again, he continued on to the second staircase without even pausing to see the outcome of his action.

The red-haired gang leader, caught off balance, rolled and tumbled all the way down the stairs, bringing down many of the bellowing rabble before him. He came to a halt when he crashed into the Head, who had come rushing out of his office to investigate the cause of the noise.

The Head stumbled and fell, whacked the bridge of his nose sickeningly hard on the edge of the hall table, and lost his temper.

"What in the world are you *idiotic children* playing at?" he roared, bowed in anguish with his nose cupped in his hands. "Fooling about on the stairs like that!"

The red-haired gang leader had jarred his shoulder very painfully, but he had not lost his uncanny instinct for making the maximum amount of trouble out of any situation. Also, he had noticed the friendliness that seemed to be growing between Indigo and Tom and he did not like it. So he eyed the rabble menacingly and replied, "I wasn't fooling about, sir. Indigo Casson pushed me."

"I did not!" shouted Indigo in surprise. "It was . . ."

Indigo stopped suddenly and looked around. Tom was nowhere in sight. "I didn't see who it was," he finished lamely.

That did not matter, because at least half the rabble, it seemed, had miraculously witnessed the whole thing: Indigo Casson pushing their leader down the stairs.

In the past all the rabble would have seen, but times were changing. A few people, David (still blueish with chalk dust), Marcus and Josh, and one or two others, no longer followed their leader quite as blindly as they had in the past. They shuffled uncomfortably when questioned and said they had not noticed anything.

In the middle of all the fuss Tom strolled up, his hands in his pockets and his eyebrows raised.

"Tom," said the Head, his nose already swelling and his eyes still streaming. "Do you happen to know who pushed this boy down the stairs?"

Tom, who knew nothing of the red-haired gang leader's inspired accusation, took his ball from his pocket and bounced it with elaborate unconcern right under the Head's aching nose. Then he asked insolently, "What does it matter? So long as somebody did!"

Indigo stared at Tom in astonishment. Never for one moment had he imagined that Tom would not say at once, "It was me!"

Tom noticed Indigo staring at him and asked, "Feeling blue, Indigo?"

The red-haired gang leader laughed.

"Tom Levin, put that ball away!" thundered the Head, who until that moment had been outraged to the point of speechlessness. "Indigo Casson wait outside my office! The rest of you get off to your classes! *Now,* not when you feel like it!"

Darling Daddy, wrote Rose grumpily that night:

> This is Rose.
> Saffy says everyone says it is <u>Indigo's</u> fault that their Head has two black eyes and a swelled-up nose.
> Love from Rose.
> P.S. Sarah who is here says tell you love from wheelchair woman too.

Rose's father telephoned especially to tell Rose not to call Sarah Wheelchair Woman.

"That's what she called herself," protested Rose. "She thought of it! Aren't you worried about what I told you about Indigo and the Head?"

"What?" asked Bill. "Oh that! Two black eyes and a swollen nose! I don't think I can believe that one, Rose darling! It doesn't sound like Indigo to me!"

"What are you doing this weekend?"

"Paris probably. Poor old Dad! It will be horribly expensive. What about you?"

"Not Paris," said Rose.

It was a very bad week. Indigo spent it waiting for Tom to explain his unreasonable behavior. Tom spent it sulking. Almost as soon as he had spoken, he had regretted mentioning his horseback-riding mother. He felt he had made a fool of himself, and he missed Indigo, who left him alone.

It was not until Friday that David told him exactly what the red-haired gang leader had said when he picked himself up at the bottom of the stairs.

Tom was no great believer in heroic self-sacrifice, but nevertheless he went to the Head (whose black eyes were now at their multicolored peak of perfection) and said, "If that red-haired moron told you Indigo Casson pushed him down the stairs on Monday he was lying. It was me."

The Head was also no believer in heroics, but he was pleased with Tom for coming forward, and so he said quite amiably (for him), "Well, well. Time is a great healer. This is a board meeting. Get out, and next time knock!"

Tom got out, hunted down Indigo, and bounced his ball off the back of his head before he even knew anyone was behind him.

"Oh, it's you!" said Indigo.

"Why didn't you tell the Head it was me who shoved that prat down the stairs?" Tom demanded indignantly, and Indigo replied, just as indignantly, "What do you think I am?"

Tom bounced his ball around for a bit, not answering, and then flashed one of his sudden, lightning smiles.

"You see me go around David with the blue chalk on Monday?" he asked.

"Yes. I told Rose."

"How is old Rose?" asked Tom politely.

"She says I've got to get you to come round to our house. Why don't you come tomorrow?"

Tom's eyebrows went up very high.

"Or are you doing something else? Going to the music shop?"

"What's the point?" asked Tom resignedly. "They know I haven't got any money. I was going to the library."

"Oh."

"I was going to find the way up on to the roof."

"What?"

"There's always a way on to a roof like that," said Tom. "There has to be. For maintenance."

"But what's so special about the library roof?"

"I like to get up high," said Tom, and Indigo remembered the fire escape, and the multistory car park, and the sound of music that had seemed to come from the sky when he and Rose visited Tom at home.

"You come with me," said Tom, "and then I'll come to your house afterward."

"You want me to come with you?"

"Why not?"

"Will you bring your guitar when you come? And show Rose that thing with the chalked ball? She'd love it."

Tom's eyes narrowed a little. He said, "Only if you'll climb up to the library roof with me first."

"I bet it isn't possible."

"Well, maybe it isn't," agreed Tom. "But I'm going to find out. Catch! How could you miss that? Try again! Tomorrow, then, at ten. Okay?"

"Okay," said Indigo.

Chapter Ten

ROSE WAS NOT PLEASED WHEN SHE HEARD THAT TOM'S plans for Saturday morning did not include a visit to the music shop. She said, "They'll think he does not want it anymore."

"They'll have more sense than that," said Indigo.

Rose did not think so. Therefore early on Saturday morning she dragged Eve out of bed and persuaded her to fit in a visit to town before the beginning of her class at the college.

"Rose darling!" protested Eve sleepily as Rose handed her toast, her shoes, and the car keys and pushed her out of the door.

At the music shop Rose was recognized at once by the kind assistant. Eve propped herself up in the doorway for five more minutes of dozing, and Rose took the black guitar, sat down on Tom's stool and solemnly tested the strings.

"Couldn't he come?" asked the assistant sympathetically.

"No," said Rose, strumming away. "But he still wants it, so don't you go selling it without him!"

"I'm afraid we can't promise . . . ," began the assistant, and then shut up because Rose was glaring so fiercely at him.

"Are you thinking of learning to play yourself?" he asked.

"I *am* playing," said Rose, "aren't I?"

"Yes indeed. Yes, of course you are! American, isn't he, your friend?"

"Yes."

"Over here for long?"

Rose stared at him. Until then it had not really occurred to her that Tom was not in England forever and ever. But of course he was not. She knew it really, she just had not thought of it.

"Till summer," she said.

"I didn't realize he'd be going back so soon."

"Soon?" asked Rose, startled. "Summer isn't soon!"

"Well, it's June now, isn't it?" asked the assistant reasonably. "Not that it feels like it by the weather! Will you be all right there for a minute or two by yourself?"

"Yes," said Rose, but she bent low over the guitar

so that he could not see her face, and she plucked the strings more and more slowly.

Meanwhile, Eve had fallen completely asleep standing up, like a horse. When someone pushed through the shop door behind her, she woke up, rubbed her eyes, and exclaimed in astonishment, "Rose darling! What *are* you doing?"

"I'm trying out this guitar," answered Rose. "I've finished now, anyway."

"Well, give it back to the man and say thank you!"

Rose did as she was told without protesting, but out in the street she could not help asking, "Have you got any money with you, Mummy?"

"Mmmm," said Eve, digging around in her huge, painty canvas shoulder bag. "Yes, I think so, darling. Yes, here's my purse."

"I mean spare money. That you don't want for anything else. Not the money that you need for food and things."

"I'm sure I have. We can't possibly need food *again*! I seem to be always buying the stuff! How much do you want?"

"How much have you got?"

Eve obligingly stopped in the street and inspected.

"Twenty pounds in notes," she said, peering into her purse, "and all this junk."

She tipped the purse to show the collection of coins, paint tube lids, beads, and broken earrings that it contained, and then passed it to Rose, saying cheerfully, "There you are, darling! Help yourself."

"Thank you," said Rose. "Would you say 'Help yourself' if it was four hundred and fifty pounds?"

"If I could. But I'm afraid it isn't. Nothing like."

"No," agreed Rose sadly, and she closed it up again and placed it gently back into her mother's bag.

"What did you want four hundred and fifty pounds for?"

"That black guitar."

"Goodness," said Eve. "Is that what it costs? That's more than I've ever spent on anything in my life! That's four hundred and fifty tubes of paint, if you buy squashed ones! It can't possibly be worth so much!"

Rose did not argue because she knew she could never make her mother understand. Eve, who happily bought her clothes from charity shops and market stalls, painted her pictures on Bill's old canvases, carted home furniture that people had dumped into trash bins to throw away, and measured her cash in terms of squashed tubes of paint, could not be expected to understand that one secondhand guitar might cost four hundred and fifty pounds. Rose found herself suddenly longing for her father. He was quite different. His wallet bulged with credit cards, and he habitually carried around at least four hundred and fifty pounds' worth of accessories in his jacket pockets.

"When is Daddy coming home?" she asked.

"Goodness knows," said Eve casually. "He's so busy. Paris this weekend, he says."

"I know. What's Paris like?"

"Wonderful," said Eve. "Perfect! I spent a summer there once. A lot of us shared a squat out of town (that's a place where you can live for free, darling, as long as the owners don't come home), and I used to do sketches for tourists outside this little café, and they would buy me coffee and things in exchange."

"Daddy said Paris was very, very expensive," remarked Rose.

"No," said Eve thoughtfully. "No. Well, I didn't spend any money there anyway! Of course, it was before I met Daddy! Are you going to tell me what you wanted that guitar for?"

"You'll laugh."

"I won't. Tell me."

"For Tom."

Eve looked at Rose, and she did not laugh. She understood about hearts, even if she did not understand about money. She put an arm around Rose and hugged her tight.

While Rose and her mother were in the music shop, Indigo was lurking around the main entrance of the town library, waiting for Tom to turn up and trying to look inconspicuous.

He felt like a suspicious character. He felt as if the words LIBRARY CLIMBER were written across his head. For this reason, and also because the computer games shop along the road was a Saturday meeting place for the red-haired gang leader and his friends, he could not wait openly on the pavement. The gang and its accompanying rabble still gave him a sick, helpless feeling in his stomach, and it was worst for him when he encountered them out of school. So Indigo kept in close to the library walls and only went out into the open every now and then to crane his neck back as far as it would go and look up. He pretended to himself that he was interested in the pigeons that circled overhead, but really he was measuring in his mind the height of the library roof.

It was very high indeed, he decided.

The library was a new building, and some people in town were very proud of it, claiming that it reminded them of Sydney Opera House. It was built of white slabs of concrete, with a flat roof from which rose seven large skylights of glass and steel shaped like enormous prisms. Indigo was gazing at them and thinking how cold the pigeons looked when someone behind him demanded casually, "Feeling blue, Indigo?"

Indigo jumped and spun around.

Tom answered his own question, "Yes. He's feeling blue!"

Tom's battered guitar case was strapped across his shoulders and he was leaning against a telephone pole, watching Indigo watching the pigeons. He lifted his eyebrows at Indigo, and Indigo laughed and his spirits rose unexpectedly.

"Look at that!" Tom said, and swung around so that Indigo could see the back of his guitar case. It was dirty and splattered and stamped with a large muddy footprint.

"One of those fools who trail round school thinking they are *so* cool came up behind me. Kicked as hard as he could."

"What did you do?"

"Shoved him under a bus!" said Tom sarcastically. "I didn't do anything! What do you think I could do with this on my back and the whole crowd of them watching? I don't know where they are now. They disappeared a while ago."

"They'll be in the games shop," said Indigo. "Look!"

He nodded down the street to where the red-haired gang leader stood smiling at them from a shop doorway. When he saw them looking he made a rude gesture and disappeared inside.

"Hold this!" commanded Tom, unstrapping his guitar. "It won't take a minute!"

"Tom, don't . . . ," began Indigo, but Tom was already sprinting back down the street. As Indigo watched he stuck his head in the games shop doorway and yelled, "Shoplifting again, Red Head? You crook!" so loudly that every single person within sight turned and stared.

"Tom!" exclaimed Indigo, in agony between laughter and fear. "He'll have you for that!"

"He'll have to find me first," said Tom, taking back his guitar case and tenderly rubbing off the muddy marks. "Look what they did! They wouldn't have cared if they'd smashed it!"

"Thanks for bringing it."

"That was the bargain," said Tom. "Half the bargain! You've got to come on to the roof now! So let's go! Before it rains and the glass gets all slippery."

Indigo glanced up in horror at the seven enormous skylights and hoped he had misheard. Tom was already leading the way inside, through the turnstiles, skirting the grubby seats where old men sat in cold weather, and then passing the ramp that wound down to the windowless basement where children's books were kept.

"These are the foothills!" he told Indigo as they crossed the seething wilderness of Adult Fiction, "and that's the summit!"

He pointed upward, to where far overhead, lighting the main staircase, the huge central skylight soared above them.

Together they climbed the stairs to the first floor (Newspapers, Periodicals, and General Reference) and then up again to the second floor (Reference Only).

"Not so many people here," observed Indigo, looking back down the stairwell to the crowds below.

"No," agreed Tom. "Shows we're getting higher!"

A friendly librarian spotted Tom's guitar and smiled and said, "Hello boys! Music is up on level three."

"Thank you," said Tom.

The whole of the third floor was devoted to music. Compact discs and LPs by the thousand. Manuscript music by the mile. Shabby instruments donated by dead musicians unguarded in open cabinets. Indigo thought if anything could slow Tom down it would be these, but they had no effect at all.

"Very nice," he said, hurrying past. He did not pause to look at anything until a curling poster of a man in a hat caught his eye. Then he stopped and said, "Hey, see who's here in England! It's old Bob!"

"Oh yes," said Indigo, trying to sound as if he knew what Tom was talking about.

Tom was not deceived. "That's Bob Dylan!" he told Indigo. "Have you never heard of Bob Dylan?" And then, when Indigo's face revealed that this was (unbelievably) the case, he continued, "That's like not having heard of . . . not having heard of . . ."

"Scotland?" suggested Indigo.

"No! Where's Scotland? *Star Wars!* Yogi Bear! . . . Well, never mind! I'll tell you who loves Bob Dylan. My father. He's got that exact same poster! He's this really old, *really old,* hippy old rock star!"

"I thought he was a baseball-playing astronaut!" remarked Indigo.

"What *planet* are you on, Indigo?" demanded Tom incredulously. *"Bob Dylan* is a hippy old rock star, not my father! My father . . . You were being funny, right? Come on! Where next?"

They looked around them. The main staircase had stopped, but the central skylight was still high overhead.

"There's more rooms up there," said Tom, gazing upward. "There must be another staircase somewhere. Through a side door, maybe . . . There!"

He pointed to a door labeled with an upward pointing arrow and the words TO LECTURE ROOM 1. Sure enough, there was another staircase behind it. They slipped through and climbed again and came to an empty corridor barred halfway along by a notice board that read: QUIET! EXAMINATIONS IN PROGRESS.

Tom and Indigo paused. There was a sound of voices and a violin being played.

"Must be music exams!" murmured Indigo.

"Good," said Tom. "We have the perfect disguise! Now, how do they get out onto the roof?"

"Through there, I bet," said Indigo, nodding to a door at the end of the corridor marked STAFF ONLY.

"That's it," agreed Tom. "We're on our way now!"

With Indigo following he tiptoed past the notice board and had just got his hand on the STAFF ONLY door handle when it was opened from the other side. A man came out.

Tom gave a big sigh and the man said, "Why don't musicians look out of their windows in the mornings?"

"I don't know," said Tom.

"Because if they did they'd have nothing to do in the afternoons! You should be in here, young man!"

He ushered them back along the corridor into an empty room.

"Shouldn't be too long!" he remarked pleasantly. "Run through a few scales while you wait! Good luck!"

"It's all part of the journey!" said Tom when his footsteps had died away. "Let's try again!"

This time they made it through the door unchallenged, past a small coffee room, past a fire exit, and past a cupboard helpfully labeled KEYS.

"Tom!" said Indigo, shocked, as Tom opened the cupboard, pocketed the bunch of keys tagged CARE-TAKER, and shut the door again, all in a second.

"Trust me!" said Tom. "I'm a musician!"

"Then you are not where you should be!" boomed a voice from behind, and they were swept down upon yet again, this time by a huge bearded man who whisked them back into their waiting room and stood leaning on the door while he asked, "All tuned up?"

"No."

"Better get on with it then."

Tom's face was so funny at this second setback that Indigo could not stop laughing. Tom ignored him, got out his guitar, and solemnly tuned up.

"Stop laughing!" the bearded librarian ordered Indigo. "You'll make him nervous! I'm going to have to leave you both. You stay put till you're called, and no messing about! Nice old guitar."

Tom looked up quickly to see if he was joking and said, "The neck is warped."

"Oh. Right."

"And the tuning pegs slip and the back is split."

"That's a shame."

"It got really wet one time you see."

151

"Oh dear," said the librarian, edging away.

"In a thunderstorm. And see that mark on the back?"

"I'm afraid I must leave you now!"

"Lightning did that. It was struck by lightning."

"What appalling luck," said the librarian and nipped out of the door before Tom could tell him anything else.

"Now!" said Tom, and this time they managed it, through the staff door, past the key cupboard, and round a corner. Then up a narrow stair to a little locked doorway. Here Tom got out his stolen bunch of keys, found the one marked ROOF, and a moment later they were out in the open at last.

The library roof was flat, with the skylights crossing the center like a range of glass mountains. A shifting, chilly wind was blowing, and the clouds, Indigo decided, were uncomfortably close. He backed against the little door they had come through and tried not to think about how high up they were.

Tom was exploding with a combination of sky, success, and anarchy. He yelled, "Whoo hoo! Here we are!" and spun madly around and around. "See! We made it!" he called upward to the ragged clouds. He unstrapped his guitar case and lay spread-eagled on his back under the windy sky and shouted, "Hello, airplanes!" He ran around the parapet, high on height, scooting the pigeons off the edge, telling them, "Fly, little birdies!"

Then he called, "Come on, Indigo! Let's look down!"

A knee-high parapet ran around the edge of the roof. Tom skidded across to it, knelt down, and hung over to his waist, calling, "Hello, little people!" to the passers-by down below. "I can see the music shop!" he called over his shoulder to Indigo.

"Can you?"

"If I stretch over really far! There's someone looking at the guitars in the window. . . . Hey!"

Tom jumped up so suddenly he nearly lost his balance, and Indigo felt his stomach turn over.

"Don't you buy my guitar!" bawled Tom down to the street below, and to Indigo he explained casually, "They just went in!"

"I wish you'd get away from that edge!" said Indigo.

"If he comes out with my guitar," said Tom, dropping back down to his knees, "I'm gonna jump off this roof and grab it out of his hands before he knows where I've come from!"

Then for the first time Tom seemed to notice that Indigo was not enjoying himself. He looked more closely, and saw that Indigo looked . . . not worried, thought Tom . . . not worried . . . bored?

"What's the matter?" he asked with his eyebrows lifted high.

Indigo could not seem to speak. Also his knees felt terrible, and his head was swimming. The sight of Tom prancing about at the edge of the parapet made him feel as if cold water was pouring down his skin.

"Come here and watch this ball," said Tom, ever the entertainer, determined that Indigo should not be bored. "See how high it bounces!"

He produced a ball from his pocket, knelt down on the parapet, leaned over, dropped it, and then almost toppled over the edge stretching to see it land. Terrified, Indigo lurched forward and grabbed his ankles, pulling him backward as hard as he could.

"Ow!" shouted Tom as his shirt bunched up and his bare stomach grazed the rough sill of the parapet. "Let go! Ouch!"

His head came down with a crack on the

stonework and Indigo stopped pulling. Tom glared at him and asked, "This you being funny again?"

Then he looked properly at Indigo, who had turned a horrible, clammy, pale greenish-gray color, and said, "You're scared."

Indigo was hunched against one of the skylights with his head between his knees. He was breathing deeply, blowing in and out like someone who has nearly drowned.

"Scared!" repeated Tom, and he waited for Indigo to reply, "What? Me? Scared?" and then perhaps describe all the higher, wilder, infinitely more dangerous heights that he, Indigo, had scaled in the past. That was what Tom would do, if he were Indigo.

Indigo did not say a word.

"Scared!" said Tom for the third time, and this time Indigo looked up with dark, unfocused eyes and said, "Yep. Don't go near the edge anymore, will you?"

If any other person (except possibly Rose) had said that to Tom it would have been the signal for him to begin balancing tricks along the edge of the parapet. There was no need, though, to pretend with Indigo. Indigo did not pretend with him.

So Tom said (amazing himself), "I won't go

near the edge anymore. Don't worry. You'll be okay."

Indigo nodded.

"You'll be fine," said Tom reassuringly.

Tom was beginning to feel fine himself; he was beginning to feel really good. He felt like the leader of an expedition, taking care of his team. It had been hard the week before to accept the responsibility of Rose, to get her from the music shop to the library without being squashed on the road, but that was because he had never done such a thing before. Now he was experienced. It was no longer the first time. He said to Indigo, "You just relax. You'll be all right with me."

Indigo raised his sick face and managed a bit of a smile. Tom was pleased.

"You keep your head down till you feel better. There's no rush. I'll be right here."

He settled against the skylight opposite Indigo's and took out his guitar.

Time went by. It was hard to play, all hunched up against a sloping surface. Cautiously Tom stood up. He strummed gently, picking out chords and humming a little. It was a pity there was nothing to sit on, up on the roof, but he managed to get comfortable, hitching himself up against the glass. Watching Indigo all the while, he searched around for a tune, remembered the poster on the library wall, grinned, and began to sing properly.

> *"Don't look down yet, Indigo,*
>> *if people passing by . . ."*

"Listen, Indy!" he paused to say. "This is a Bob Dylan tune!"

> *"See you plastered on the sky . . ."*

The comfortable place he had found happened to be the top of the highest skylight. He had climbed it backward, without even noticing.

> *"They will know that you can't fly,*
>> *and start complaining!*
> *And I think we would find it hard*
>> *to quickly disappear*
> *No place to hide up here . . .*
> *On this jingle-jangle morning . . .*
>> *now it's raining . . ."*

Indigo, who was already smiling, looked up in surprise and then began to laugh, as the rain, that had begun falling without him even noticing, suddenly became twice as heavy.

"We should go up that church tower one day," remarked Tom, seeing Indigo had come back to life again. "That would cure you of being scared of heights! I can see miles from here! Right across to school. I'm definitely going to climb school before I have to go. . . . What's the matter now?"

"What do you think you look like from underneath?" demanded Indigo.

"What d'you mean, from underneath?" asked Tom, and then he looked down and saw exactly what Indigo meant. The skylight glass was blurry and reinforced with a net of steel, but he could still see movement through it. Dozens of little colored blobs, dozens of people moving up and down the library stairs, any of whom might look up at any time and notice that there was someone on the library roof.

"Whoops!" said Tom, sliding down the glass in a flash. "Time to go! Okay now?"

"Yes."

"Let's run then!"

One minute they had been under the sky, and the next they were sauntering down the corridor past the room where the music exams were still taking place, the roof door relocked, the keys replaced, the staff door passed unchallenged.

Then they were on the floor below. ("Say bye-bye to Bob!" said Tom. "Bye, Bob," said Indigo obligingly.)

On the next floor down the librarian who had advised Tom to practice his scales smiled at them and asked, "How did it go?"

"Fine," Tom told him, and he nodded and said, "I knew it would!"

In no time at all they were back in the street again. Tom looked up at the highest skylight and said, "There's a pigeon sitting where I was sitting!"

Indigo looked down and found Tom's ball, rolled into the gutter.

"Must be our lucky day!" said Tom.

"Catch!" said Indigo.

He threw the ball and Tom caught it. Then Tom threw it back, and Indigo missed, and Tom said, "How could anyone miss a catch like that?"

"Let's go and find Rose," said Indigo.

Chapter Eleven

WHILE TOM AND INDIGO WERE ON THE LIBRARY ROOF, ROSE was in her mother's Saturday-morning art class, which this week was designing T-shirts with Attitude.

There was an undercurrent of discontent in the air. Even Eve, who defended her students no matter what, was forced to admit they were not at their best on Saturday mornings.

"It's the Friday nights, poor darlings," she said, in explanation of their uncreative grumpiness, understanding that the consequences of Friday nights were beyond anyone's control.

Will I have Friday nights, wondered Rose as she gazed idly around the college art room.

Yes.

The atmosphere in the room was catching, and Rose began another disgruntled letter to her father.

Darling Daddy,

This is Rose.

Mummy has made me a T-shirt that says permanent Rose with iron-on letters to show everyone how to do it.

Rose paused and looked around. On the board at the front was a list of words and phrases which her mother considered not suitable for use in college T-shirt design. She had been asked about some of them so often that in the end she had started a blacklist of banned words to which everyone could refer. Every time someone thought of a new one she unflinchingly wrote it down.

"Have you learned any you didn't know before?" one student asked her.

"No, darling," said Eve, a little wistfully. "Not for years and years and years."

Rose read through the list, and turned back to her letter.

These are the words I learned to spell in Mummy's art class today, she wrote, and sighed a little as she began the tedious job of copying from the board. She wished she had some new crisis to report. Sometimes she was afraid she would never find anything bad enough to bring her father home again. She had less and less hope that he would ever read one of her letters, exclaim in horror, and come storming to the rescue.

Beside her, a boy with expensive-looking hair extensions and dark sunglasses was finishing embossing the words CRIME PAYS in fluorescent pink on a black T-shirt. Rose watched as he chopped off the sleeves ("You don't want sleeves," he explained kindly when he saw her looking), stripped off his old shirt, and pulled on the new one instead.

"Are you a burglar?" she asked him hopefully, thinking of the black guitar.

"Do I look like a burglar?" he demanded indignantly.

"Yes."

"People always jump to conclusions," he said crossly, and yanked his T-shirt off again and screwed it into a ball.

"Can I have it if you don't want it?" asked Rose.

"If you like."

The class came to an end at last. Students either wore their work or tossed it into the bin. They fled the room, groaning with relief, and suddenly Eve and Rose were alone.

Eve swept up scraps of cloth and transfer paper from the floor. Rose said, "You don't want sleeves," hacked through the ones on her Permanent Rose T-shirt, hauled it on, and cheered up because Indigo was bringing Tom home that day.

Then they carried the box of spare shirts out to the car, lost the car keys and found them again (on a thong around Eve's neck), and were just driving out of the car park when Eve exclaimed, "The iron!," skidded to a halt, and ran back inside to switch it off.

Three minutes later they reached the same point again and screeched into a U-turn. "That awful list!" cried Eve, and rushed back inside once more to clean the board. She came back out, started the engine, and asked, "Did I close the windows?"

Rose nodded her head, and to prevent any more delays, stuffed her fingers into her ears and screwed her eyes tight shut.

When she opened them again they were home,

and Indigo and Tom were waving to her through the car window.

"Hello, Permanent Rose," said Tom.

Indigo made everyone a late lunch. It was an afternoon of revelations for Tom, and the first of them was Indigo making lunch. He made bacon rolls and maple syrup pancakes, flipping the pancakes ceiling-high, as Caddy had taught him to do the week before, and catching them perfectly in the frying pan each time.

"How come you can catch pancakes and you can't catch a ball?" demanded Tom.

"Practice," said Indigo.

A pile of pancakes was carried to the shed for Eve. Tom volunteered to take them because as soon as Eve had climbed out of the car she had murmured, "Must see if my cats are still sticky," and sloped off down the garden path.

She did not return and Tom became curious. He wondered how sticky the cats must be to keep her away for so long. He assumed he would find her diligently rubbing them clean. Therefore he was very startled when he arrived with the pancakes to find Eve comfortably asleep on a faded pink sofa, and not a sticky cat in sight. He shook her awake and said, "I've brought you some pancakes, and I think your cats have escaped."

"Darling," moaned Eve, pulling an ancient striped dressing gown over her head, "not *another* surreal conversation, *please*!" and fell asleep again.

Tom marched out of the shed feeling indignant on Indigo's behalf. At home in America he was accustomed to any contributions of his own to family life (not that he had made many for the last year or two) being given terrific applause. An offering as spectacular as pancakes would probably end up in a glass case. He returned to the kitchen and there was Sarah, who had shared the bacon rolls and pancakes, propped up against the kitchen sink, scrubbing greasy plates.

It was the first time Tom had seen Sarah out of her wheelchair, and he found the sight rather disconcerting.

"Should she be doing that?" he whispered to Indigo.

"It's her turn," said Indigo, quite callously, Tom thought. He was not a bit surprised when a moment later Sarah suddenly started wailing, "Oh my legs! My legs! Take the dishcloth quick, Tom! Everything's going dim and blurry!"

Tom took the dishcloth at once, and was washing

up for ages before he realized Saffron and Sarah and Rose were drying the plates and passing them back to him over and over again.

"Rose!" said Tom reproachfully.

"You haven't even looked at my picture," said Rose.

"I have."

"Not carefully."

Tom put down the dishcloth and came across the kitchen and looked at Rose's picture properly. He looked at it and looked at it, and said at last, "You did all this yourself?"

Rose nodded.

"Whew," said Tom.

Rose began to introduce him to the people that mattered in her life.

"That's Caddy, who is at college in London. She'll be coming home soon for the summer. That's Derek-from-the-camp, who used to be her boyfriend. This is Michael, who says he's going to marry her. There's Sarah's mother bringing Sunday lunch in a boat, and that's Sarah next to Saffron. And that's our mother asleep beside the chimney, and me next to Indigo. He can't fall off. . . . That's your father's rocket."

"It is?"

"And over there is your mother. Taking care of the bears. That island is America. From a distance."

"Looks just like it," said Tom.

"And over there is where I started to try and draw you. It's the best place because you can lean back against the chimney—"

"It used to be mine," interrupted Sarah. "I was cleaned off! I am treated very badly in this house!"

". . . But I can't get the guitar right," continued Rose, ignoring Sarah. "I can't make your hands look like they are holding it properly."

Tom looked around for his guitar case, but Indigo was already passing it to him. He took his guitar out and sat with his hands holding it properly. Rose looked at him carefully and began to draw.

Rose frowned with concentration and drew and drew, and Tom sat patiently all the time, playing now and then, and talking in between. Once he looked up and saw Indigo grinning at him. He raised his eyebrows and began finger-picking an intricate cascade of notes on his guitar.

"Play that again," said Sarah. "It sounded gorgeous."

Tom played it again, and was happy. Not wild, up-in-the-sky happy, but ordinarily, peacefully, content. It was such an unusual feeling that he noticed it was there.

After a while Sarah and Saffron left for Sarah's house, and Rose grew tired of drawing. Tom began to teach Indigo how to hold a guitar, and Rose, remembering her clumsiness in the music shop that morning, came to look too. The humming darkness in the opening behind the strings intrigued her, and she asked, "What's inside the hole?"

"Nothing," Tom answered. "Well, just an old label . . . See?"

"What does it say?"

"*Admira*," Tom told her, not needing to look. "That's the make of the guitar."

"And the little letters underneath?"

"*Fabricado en España,*" said Tom, "I think." He bent over his guitar to peer at the faded writing and caught a breath of the smell of the inside, pungent with wood and dust and varnish, faintly musty. "*Fabricado en España . . .*"

His voice faded as he spoke. He took a deeper breath. The inside of his guitar smelled of home so piercingly that all at once he was three thousand miles away. He would not have been surprised to hear the hum of the

traffic or the sound of familiar doors opening and closing. He could have sworn he heard a baby wail.

He could not have been more startled if he had
seen a ghost.

When Tom came out of his daze it was to find
Rose and Indigo staring at him in astonishment.

"Your hands are shaking," said Rose.

"I was spooked," he said apologetically. "I was . . .
It was really weird. . . . Smell inside my guitar!"

They sniffed obligingly, but shook their heads.
The smell meant nothing to them.

"It gave me an awful feeling," said Tom. "Shivery . . ."

It had smelled of resentment. And the helpless
anger that comes from being towed into a life where
you do not want to be. And months and months and
months of sulking in his bedroom. It smelled of closed
doors behind which were whispered strategies to make
him, Tom, the family problem, give in. And be happy.

Back at home in America they had tried very hard
indeed to make Tom give in and be happy.

"You have tried much *too* hard!" his English grandmother had remarked severely when Tom's father told
her about Tom's wish to be a million miles away. "But

I don't mind taking him off your hands for a while. It will give you a break, and it won't kill Tom! He will have to go to school of course, I'm not having him hanging around underfoot all day, and he can help with the cats when he gets home. And if he likes to spend the rest of his time indulging in childish tantrums, that is quite all right with me. I am immune to tantrums!" she had said complacently. "Send him over by all means!"

So Tom, at his own request, had come to England, that being as far as could be managed to a million miles away. There he was no happier than he was in America, and considerably less comfortable. Also, at his grandmother's house he was quite spectacularly not the center of attention, although he managed to make up for that at school. And he was terribly lonely. He didn't like England, and he didn't like home. Until the Saturday afternoon when he visited the Casson house for the first time, there was no place in the world that he wanted to be.

Tom stayed all afternoon, and so late into the evening that Eve, emerging from her shed at last, kindly offered him a patch of Indigo's floor for the night.

"I'd better go," said Tom reluctantly.

"Come back tomorrow," said Indigo. "Nobody else is coming."

"Aren't they?" asked Rose, looking hopefully at Eve.

Eve shook her head and said, "I don't think so, darling. Not Daddy, anyway!"

"Bloody Daddy," said Rose.

"Rose!"

"I've told Tom about him never coming home any-more," said Rose unrepentantly, "and Tom says—"

"I'll see you tomorrow, then!" interrupted Tom loudly, and at the same time Indigo ordered, "Shut up, Rose!"

"Oh, all right," said Rose, but when Tom was gone she finished off the letter that she had started in the art class that morning. It was, she thought smugly as she drew the kisses across the bottom, the scariest yet.

> Tom says one day soon you will come back
> and say Surprise, Surprise. This Is My New Wife
> and This Is My New Baby.
> And expect us to be pleased.
> Love, Rose.

It was after dark when Tom got back to his grand-mother's house, so late that she had been worrying.

"I know communication is not your strong point, but you could have telephoned," she complained. "Where have you been?"

"At Indigo's. I met him in town."

"The tall thin boy with the baby sister?"

"She's not a baby."

"I expect she was once. What is she called?"

"Rose," said Tom. "They're all called after different colors. Their mother got them off a paint chart, they told me. Cadmium, Saffron, Indigo, and Rose."

"What very nice names!"

"Their parents are artists," Tom told her, pleased to have someone to talk to about his new friends. "Their mother paints pictures in a shed at the end of the garden but their father is in London. He doesn't come home much anymore. And Saffron is really their cousin. She's adopted."

"There are all sorts of families," commented his grandmother, "and most of them seem to get on together, one way or another."

Tom was silent.

"Bring Rose to see my cats one day. The Burmese. I'm sure she'd enjoy that. Although you will have to explain that I am not a witch. I expect she will be disappointed!"

Tom looked up at her in astonishment. She had never seemed so friendly before.

"All sorts of families," she repeated, her eyes on the clearing sky. "You'll learn. And now come in and have your supper."

When Rose's letter arrived in London it worried her father so much that he telephoned Eve that same day.

"You would not believe the words she says she has learned," he began, and read them out to her.

"Oh," said Eve laughing. "I remember. My list of banned words! I wrote them on the board for my Saturday-morning art class. We were designing T-shirts. She went to school in one of them this morning. Right down past her knees with 'Crime Pays' in big pink letters across the front. . . ."

"Whatever did she look like?" asked Bill, appalled.

"Well, not terribly tidy," admitted Eve. "Although Sarah and Saffron had managed to stretch her hair into two very darling little plaits . . ."

"Crime pays!"

"Well, of course Rose knows that is not true," said

Eve soothingly. "Or hardly ever. Not usually. Although I must say some of my students do seem to find—"

"I wish you would not take Rose to your classes," said Bill irritably. "Look at the language she has picked up! And if you ask me, what you teach is not exactly . . ."

Eve gently put the telephone receiver down and began to hum while she sorted through the contents of her handbag. After a couple of minutes she picked it up again, said quickly, "You are absolutely right, darling! Must dash!" and hung up.

"Who was that?" asked Rose, coming in.

"Daddy."

"Oh."

"He loved your letter," said Eve, improvising rapidly.

"Loved it?"

"He was very interested in the T-shirts. And the list of words (which I know you would never ever use, Rose darling)."

"What else did he say?"

"I didn't quite catch the end."

"Is he coming to see us?"

"Absolutely definitely," said Eve, hugging Rose.

Chapter Twelve

"THERE ARE ALL SORTS OF FAMILIES," TOM'S GRANDMOTHER had remarked, and over the following few weeks Tom became part of the Casson family, as Michael and Sarah and Derek-from-the-camp had done before him.

He immediately discovered that being a member of the family was very different from being a welcome friend. If you were a Casson family member, for example, and Eve drifted in from the shed asking, "Food? Any ideas? Or shall we not bother?" then you either joined in the search of the kitchen cupboards or counted the money in the housekeeping jam jar and calculated how many pizzas you could afford. Also, if you were a family member you took care of Rose, helped with homework (Saffron and Sarah were very strict about homework), unloaded the washing machine, learned to fold up Sarah's wheel-chair, hunted for car keys, and kept up the hopeful theory that in the event of a crisis Bill Casson would disengage himself from his artistic life in London and rush home to help.

Some of these things Tom understood naturally, and some were explained to him by Indigo, to whom they were a part of life. Indigo, Tom was beginning to realize, was no fool, even if he was afraid of high places and the red-haired gang leader and his rabble.

In those chilly, light, unsummery days the red-haired gang leader never seemed to be far away.

He was often unhappy.

One cause of the red-haired gang leader's unhappiness was Tom. Tom's arrogance hurt him like a pain in his heart. Another reason, even worse, was the fact that he had yet to win his long battle with Indigo. It seemed very unfair that he had tried so hard, and for so long, and yet he still had not won. He could not understand it. He could not understand how, even at the height of his power, when Indigo had walked among them as nervous and alone as a daylight ghost, he had not won.

The fact that Indigo, of all fighters the most

hopeless, should endure for so long, tormented the red-haired gang leader like a fever.

He began to urge his rabble on to new levels of achievement.

This was hard work. The rabble needed far more encouraging than they had done in the past. Three of them, Josh and Marcus and David, were almost useless. They disappeared whenever there was any dirty work to be done. Also, it seemed to their leader that others were beginning to copy them.

In daylight the red-haired gang leader laughed at this ridiculous thought, but at nighttime he lay awake in bed, tossing and turning, reviewing the evidence.

There was very little evidence.

All the same, he began to hear mutterings behind his back.

Then he acted quickly, because his leadership meant more to him than anything else in his life. Discipline in the gang became tighter than ever, and there were many unpleasant incidents. On the other hand, loyalty was rewarded as never before.

In the past the red-haired leader had fastidiously avoided touching his adoring rabble: Now he flung his arms across their dandruffy and shambling shoulders and told them they were heroes. He gave high fives without flinching. For even the least colorful and enthusiastic he invented cryptic and flattering nicknames. His vigilant presence allowed no private meetings. He was everywhere.

When these tactics had brought his people a little more into shape again, he announced that Indigo Casson should no longer be ignored. Indigo and Tom, he explained, were now obviously a team. Indigo had been immune for long enough.

No one dared remind him of Saffron and Sarah's visit on the first morning of term. Nobody muttered rebellious thoughts to an ally. There were a few furtive glances, which the red-haired leader noted with cold and furious eyes, but that was all. Things were not as good as they had been in the glorious old days of total power, but there were still enough brave and loyal rabble members to make life quite smelly and messy and painful for Tom and Indigo in the time that followed.

"Feeling blue, Indigo?" enquired Tom sardonically, as Indigo cleaned dog mess off his jacket in the washroom at the end of a school day.

"Nope," said Indigo.

"Well you should be. Look at what you are doing!"

"It's clean again now."

"Listen. There's two of us. Let's take them on and see how many we can lay out before they knock us flat."

"It wouldn't work," said Indigo, wafting the wet patch on his jacket under the hand dryer.

"Explain! Explain! Explain!" ordered Tom, pounding Indigo between the shoulder blades with a handy tennis racket.

"The more attention you pay to them, the worse they are. I bet they'd love a chance to flatten us. They'd all join in. Rose would find out."

"So what?"

"She'd be really upset if we came home flattened."

"I think old Rose is a lot tougher than you know," remarked Tom.

"Maybe."

"A lot tougher! Let's take her with us when we go up the church tower."

"Are we going up the church tower?" asked Indigo, surprised. They had tried to do this once before and found it closed for repairs.

"Absolutely we are going up the church tower," said Tom. "It's open again. Three hundred and sixty-five steps, my grandmother says."

He bounced a ball off the ceiling and caught it with his left hand. His right one was black across the back of all four fingers from being slammed in a classroom door.

"Will you be able to play your guitar with your hand like that?" asked Indigo, looking at it.

"I think so. It's a bit stiff though. I couldn't if it was my other one."

"What'll you tell Rose?"

"I'll say I got it slammed in a door of course."

Rose finished her picture that week, adding the final touches: a glimpse of Derek-from-the-camp's motorbike through an upstairs bedroom window, an engagement ring on Caddy's hand (from Michael), and even more cruising shark fins among the waves. Over the next few days everyone who came near the house was dragged in to admire it. The milkman said she was a clever little lass. The postman said, "Well I never!" and shook her hand. Sarah's mother said it was a remarkable achievement. Sarah's father said, "Where's good old Bill?"

Rose pointed to the sharks.

Eve said it ought to be sprayed with fixative, and one Saturday lunchtime she came back from the college with three large tins of the stuff.

"I should hate it to get smudged," she explained to Rose.

Michael said, "I suppose I'd better go and buy a ring, then. What is it?"

Rose said it was a great big diamond.

Derek-from-the-camp, who had dropped in for coffee and (he told Rose) to see if Eve had fallen in love with him yet (advised by Rose, he had given up all hope of Caddy), said he knew fully paid-up artists who had never done anything to touch it.

Rose said so did she.

Then everyone helped to get the spraying done, which was an enormous undertaking. So large was the finished picture, that even with the doors and windows open, the fumes from the fixative caused Rose's admirers to retire one by one, wheezing and rubbing their burning eyes, long before the work was done. It was left to Tom, as latest member of the family, to finish the job off.

"Good man!" said Michael when Tom finally staggered into the garden, triumphantly waving the last empty can.

"So how long," asked Derek, draping a black leather arm around Eve and winking at Rose, "before you go back to the States, Tom?"

"Not for ages," snapped Rose, before Tom could answer. "Get your arm off my mother!"

"Not till summer," said Tom.

"Any day now then?" said Derek, planting a great smacking kiss on Eve's ear. *"Ouch! Rose!"*

"Serves you right," said Rose, watching with pleasure as he hobbled in painful circles around and around the lawn.

Derek pulled up the leg of his jeans to inspect the damage. "Crikey, look at that!" he moaned.

"Hideous," said Saffron, giggling.

"Couldn't you shave them or something?" asked Sarah.

"Look, Eve! Look where your daughter kicked me! A great purple bruise!"

"Mmmm," said Eve, sidling into her shed.

"Oh well," said Derek. "Rose is obviously right.

Nobody loves me. Perhaps I'd better take off for America too! Are you looking forward to getting back to civilization, Tom?"

"I told you," said Tom, a bit impatiently, "I'm not going for ages. Not till summer, I said."

"Summertime's now, mate," said Derek.

"Shouldn't you be going back to your camp?" asked Rose.

"Maybe I should," agreed Derek. "Back to my non-violent protest!"

He shook hands with Tom before he left and said he hoped they would meet up again, and catching Rose alone for a moment, he squatted down to her height and asked very kindly, "You getting sad about Tom going home, Permanent Rose?"

"No."

"That's all right then. It's a very small world, you know!"

"Is it?"

"Gets smaller all the time. You'll see."

"Does your leg still hurt?"

"Not a bit."

"Good," said Rose.

• • •

When Derek had gone Tom borrowed a handful of pastels from Rose, stood Indigo against the side of the house, and performed his ball-throwing trick. However, his heart was not really in it—his last ball nearly took off Indigo's right ear, and he dropped the catch when it bounced back.

"How could you miss that?" asked Indigo sweetly.

"Lost concentration," said Tom a little wearily.

Usually he was very good at distracting himself from the things he did not want to think about. This time it was not working so well. There was no doubt, he reluctantly admitted to himself as he watched Rose join the splodges of pastel on the wall of the house into an enormous looming skeleton, there was no doubt that time was passing.

That evening, back at his grandmother's house, Tom climbed the now familiar route out of his bedroom window and onto the porch roof. There he sat for a long time, hugging his guitar and thinking of home.

Nowadays home seemed very far away.

Tom had switched lives as completely as if he had moved to another planet. He had sent no letters and answered no telephone calls. Completely deliberately, he had turned his back and walked away.

At the airport, on that last day in America, Tom's father had said, "Nobody wants you to do this."

Tom had shrugged.

"Tom. Let's talk. It's not too late to talk."

"Talk then," Tom had replied, taking a ball out from his pocket.

"Tom, will you come back with me and have one more go at working things out?"

"No."

"That's it, then? No? That's all you have to say?"

"You work things out," Tom told him stubbornly. "It's your problem."

His father began to speak and then stopped. He touched a hand on Tom's shoulder, very lightly, like a caress.

"Any suggestions?"

Tom had not just a suggestion, but a solution. It was one he had thought of weeks before, but he had hugged it to himself and kept quiet, not wanting to be the one to put it into words. He knew his father had worked it out already.

In the old days, when Tom and his father had

been a complete family to one another, they had understood each other. Tom did not know why it was not like this anymore. He stood at the airport, fiddling with his ball while they lined up to check in his luggage, and said silently to his father in his head, "You know the answer! And I know you know."

"Tom?" his father said. "Tom, remember when we tried to do Christmas twice?"

That was an old joke between them. Tom had been six, and it was February and snowing. Christmas had been spent on the Mexican coast, and from Tom's six-year-old point of view it had been a total disaster. Sunshine and dolphins and presents on the beach were not his idea of Christmas.

Then they got back and late in the winter, the snow arrived. It seemed a waste to Tom. He had looked out at the big gray flakes tumbling past the streetlights and asked, "Why can't we do Christmas twice?"

"We can," his father had replied grandly, and they very nearly had. They had wrapped up presents and bought a turkey. They had even, with immense difficulty, found a tree. But by the time they got the tree tracked down, the snow was melting, and the place that was still selling trees was also selling Easter decorations. Tom's father was all for decorating the tree with yellow chicks and painted eggs, but Tom said that this would be wrong.

"Dad," he said reluctantly, after he had won the argument about the Easter decorations. "I don't think this will work. I don't think we can do Christmas twice!"

Then, from somewhere among the small crowd of people that had collected around them while they argued, a deep, deep voice had boomed, "The boy is right!"

Sometimes, for years after that, Tom's father would boom out, "The boy is right!" in just the same way.

That was the time they tried to do Christmas twice.

Remembering it at the crowded airport had done something to Tom. He had to turn away from the check-in queue and draw a forefinger under each eye in turn, casually, so that no one would notice.

"Don't go through with this," said his father.

At that moment Tom gave up waiting for him to put into words the solution to all the unhappiness that had brought them to this place. He said, "She could take it with her and go somewhere else. Anywhere. Just, not in our house . . ."

He paused at that point, because he could feel his father's eyes, dark and penetrating on the top of his head.

Also shocked.

Perhaps, thought Tom, in surprise, this solution had not occurred to his father. Perhaps that was why he was suddenly so silent.

When Tom spoke again it was a little more kindly. "You could visit. . . . Whenever you wanted. Whenever. That would be all right."

His father did not get angry. Or sarcastic. Just quiet and thoughtful.

Thinking about it, Tom guessed.

"It works with me and Mom," Tom had pointed out, but this was so untrue that he was forced to add, "most of the time.

"It would work," he amended, "if she didn't keep hanging on to that crummy old boyfriend. . . ."

His father said, as if he had not heard any of this, "No. That is not going to happen. That is not a solution. That is never ever . . . I can't believe you've been thinking like that, Tom! *No one* is going *anywhere*."

"I am," said Tom, more angrily than ever, and then they reached the front of the queue and the first thing he handed over to be labeled and loaded on to the plane was his guitar. Then his big bag, and then his rucksack. He did not say another word to his father.

That was what had happened the day Tom flew to England. He sat on the roof of the porch at his grand-mother's house, remembering it all. He thought of home, and he thought of Indigo and Rose.

He said out loud, "I never want to go back."

Chapter Thirteen

ROSE WAS MOPING. SHE WAS HANGING AROUND THE house, moping. She said she had "not got anything to do."

"What about painting?" asked Caddy, telephoning from London.

"My picture's finished."

"Well, you could start another. The last one was so good, everyone said so."

"Horrible Daddy didn't," said Rose gloomily. "Caddy?"

"Yes?"

"When are you going to marry Michael?"

"What! How did you know? That was supposed to be a secret! Anyway, probably not for ages."

"Where will you live?"

"Goodness knows!"

"What will you wear?"

"Probably something very tight," said Caddy, who

had given a great deal of thought to this (but no other) aspect of marriage. "And totally silver with sequins all over."

"You'll look like a fish."

"Or pink. Very bright pink?"

"You couldn't possibly," said Rose, and then suddenly brightened up because through the window she could see Indigo, and Tom with him, carrying his guitar.

"Hello, Permanent Rose!" said Tom, coming in.

"Who are you talking to?" Indigo asked.

"Caddy. Caddy, it's Indigo with Tom! Caddy doesn't know what to wear to marry Michael! Very tight silver sequins like a fish, or bright pink, but I said she couldn't possibly."

"My mother wore a cowgirl dress," remarked Tom, getting out his guitar.

"What did your father wear?" asked Indigo. "His space suit? Or just his baseball cap?"

Tom wrestled him to the ground and sat on him.

"Tell her to wear that short black sparkly thing with long gloves that she wore to Granddad's funeral," called Indigo, heaving Tom to one side.

"Tell her a cowgirl dress!" yelled Tom.

"I heard them!" said Caddy. "What awful ideas!

You think of something, Rose darling!"

Rose said she could only think of boring white lace, sticking out for miles. This exactly described the dress that Caddy had secretly longed for ever since she was five years old, so she said, "Perfect!" and rang off before Rose could explain that she had been joking.

Tom lay flat on his back on the floor with one leg bent up and the other crossed over it to rest his guitar on. He twanged the strings experimentally for a minute and then sang,

> *"Woke up this mornin'*
> *And found*
> *I was wearing*
> *Boring white lace. . . ."*

"Is that a real song?" asked Rose incredulously. "Or did you just make it up?"

"Both," said Tom, twanging away.

> *"Not the short sparkly black*
> *With the gloves*
> *Indigo loves*
> *(Feeling blue, Indigo?)"*

Indigo dropped a cushion on his face.

> *"Not silver like a fish*
>> *(sang Tom, through the cushion)*
> *Not pink*
> *Said Rose, who knows.*
> *Woke up this mornin'*
> *With a bad case*
> *Of White Lace*
> *Blues"*

Then, while Rose and Indigo were still laughing, he wandered off into a melody.

"It's suppose to sound like a harp," he told them as he played. "I learned it when I was just beginning to play, and added bits. . . . I do wish this guitar would ever stay in tune for five minutes together!"

"Perhaps it's because you're playing upside down," said Indigo.

"It's because the strings won't stay tight," said Tom. "Not to mention the back is split and the neck is warped and it's the wrong sort of guitar anyway . . . Still you better learn the right way up, Indigo. Come on, your turn!"

It was not the first guitar lesson that Indigo had been given. There had been several, some at the Casson house and some at Tom's, up on the roof of the porch.

"The perfect place," Tom had said. "You can't be worrying about the height if you're playing the guitar, and if you're playing the guitar, then obviously you're not worrying about the height!"

This was true, and it worked. Indigo grew quite comfortable with being on the roof, and he learned at a speed that astonished Tom. His fingers did not fumble, and he heard his mistakes as quickly as Tom did.

"You need to practice," said Tom. "You'd soon be really good."

The drawback to Indigo learning to play was the difficulty of sharing one guitar between two people. It meant carrying it backward and forward across town. This made Tom an obvious target for the red-haired gang leader and his rabble. One evening he was spotted, and the next he was followed. On the third he was hunted through the streets and arrived at the Cassons' filthy and breathless and more troubled than Indigo had ever seen him before.

"Two of them jumped me and some more came

up behind," he said as they examined the damage together in Indigo's bedroom. "And they got my guitar case off me and started trying to open it. If they'd realized you have to push both catches at the same time they'd have managed to. I wish it had locks."

"How did you get it back?" asked Indigo.

"I grabbed the one trying to open it by the neck and I—Hello, Rose!"

"What are you telling Indigo about?" inquired Rose suspiciously. "Why are you so muddy? And what happened to your face?"

"Nothing much. I'm so hungry! Do you think you would make me a sandwich, Rose?"

"Later."

"What about a drink?"

"Why don't you get some water from the bathroom?"

"Rose," said Indigo. "Buzz off."

"Oh, all right," said Rose.

"So anyway," continued Tom when she had gone, "I had hold of Jason, and the others were pulling at me from behind, and Jason was sort of coughing and struggling, and then someone shouted, 'Run!' And guess who'd pulled up beside us? The Head! He got out of his car and said, 'What's going on here?'

and I looked around and it was just me and Jason. Everyone else had disappeared.

"The Head just stood there, looking. Jason had terrible red marks on his throat. He looked like someone had been trying to kill him, and my nose was all bloody from where he had bashed it with his head.

"Then the Head said to Jason, 'How did you get those marks on your throat?' and Jason said, 'Didn't know I had any marks, sir,' like he couldn't care less."

"Didn't he notice your nose?" asked Indigo.

"Yes, he did then. He asked about it and I told him I'd probably been sneezing. So he said, really irritated, 'Get off home, both of you!' Then Jason went one way, and I picked up my guitar and came here."

"Did they come after you again?"

"No. I kept checking around. And every time I turned back to look, the Head was still standing there, watching. . . . He doesn't like me."

"He doesn't like anyone," said Indigo, who had been working as he listened. "I've cleaned up your case. It's a bit cracked around one of the locks, though."

"That's where they were kicking it. I know what they were going to do if they'd got it out. Drop it in the river. I heard Jason say. We were right by the bridge when they got me."

"I know that boy Jason!" announced Rose from behind the door, where she had been listening all the while. "His brother is at my school. I could beat him up for you if you like."

"Don't you dare!" ordered Indigo. "You stay out of it. It's nothing to do with you or Jason's brother!"

"What about if I beat up Jason then?"

"No, thank you, Rose," said Tom, laughing. "You leave Jason alone."

"I'm a brilliant fighter," said Rose sadly. "Why do you always leave me out?"

"We don't," said Indigo. "But you can't just go around attacking people."

"Why not?"

"Because you are just a little kid," said Tom impatiently, and oblivious to Rose's indignant glare, he took out his guitar and began tuning up.

"I'll show you a couple of chords," he said to Indigo, and began demonstrating to him how to hold his hands and move his fingers. He and Indigo soon became so absorbed that Rose grew restless. She had always assumed that playing an instrument came naturally to people, as painting did to her, and she found all this patient listening and practicing very boring indeed.

After a while she wandered off, and finding Sarah downstairs, enlisted her help to write another letter to her father.

"I'll tell you the words and you put them down," she proposed. "That'll be much faster than me writing. And we can make it really long."

"All right."

"You won't add any on or take any away?"

"Of course not. Off you go!"

"Begin, *Darling Daddy*," dictated Rose.

Darling Daddy,

This is Rose.

Very good news. Caddy is going to marry Michael. In case you have forgotten because you have not been home for so long he is the one with the ponytail and the earring that you do not like. But we do. And Caddy says she will have a white lace dress and three bridesmaids, Saffron and Sarah and me, and a big party for everyone, all her old boyfriends too. Fireworks. A band. A big tent called a marquee. But where will we put it? Carriages with white horses for us all to go to the church. Afterward Caddy and Michael will go for a holiday to Australia to visit the Great Barrier Reef. Caddy has worked it all out and Mummy says Yes She Can Of Course You Can Darling Of Course You Must Do That. Saffron said That Will Cost a Few Weeks Housekeeping and Mummy said Yes But We Do Not Need to Worry About That. DADDY WILL PAY.

Love, Rose.

Sarah, faithfully writing down every word, none added and none taken away, found this message so hilarious that Rose got cross.

"It's meant to be scary," she told her.

"It's scary," said Sarah.

When Tom went home that evening he left his guitar in Indigo's bedroom.

"It's stupid for me to keep carrying it backward and forward every day," he said.

Indigo understood. He knew that however much

Tom complained about his guitar, it was still infinitely better than no guitar at all. After that it stayed at the Casson house, and Tom spent more and more of his time there.

"I'm beginning to miss your playing," remarked Tom's grandmother one evening as they washed the supper dishes together.

"I never knew you liked it!" said Tom, astonished.

"Of course I did!"

"I could bring it back again, I suppose."

"No, no! Hardly worth it when you'll be going back so soon. The time has gone so quickly. I must say, I didn't expect it to when you first arrived."

"Neither did I." Tom paused and then asked the question that had been on his mind for some time. "Gran, could I stay a bit longer? After term ends?"

"Tom!"

"I could help you. With the cats and everything."

"But Tom, it was only ever to be until the end of term! Your father is taking time from work to come over for you. And your plane ticket is booked. . . ."

"It could be changed."

"And it's not as if . . ." She paused, not wanting

to say what she had begun to say, that it was not as if Tom had made a success of being in England. "Not as if you've been very happy here . . ."

"I am now."

"Are you?" Tom's grandmother stopped washing dishes and looked at him carefully. "Yes, perhaps you are! If it was up to me, Tom, you could stay and I should be glad to have you. But you will have to talk to your father."

Tom's face shut down as if a light had been switched off inside him.

After that the days began to go very quickly. Caddy would be home any day, which brought Eve out of her shed for an orgy of house cleaning. She helped Rose to paint all the unused space on the kitchen wall around her picture a metallic dusky gold which beautifully set off the stormy waters and the sky. Also they pushed a great many things under beds and sofas, tidied the grass of the guinea pig grave-yard, and at Rose's insistence, went shopping for food.

"Real food," said Rose sternly when Eve, sent out on her own, returned with strawberries and cherries.

"Supermarket food!" she ordered, and dragged Eve out again.

Then Caddy came home, loaded with presents, burdened with debts, and shortly after her arrival, "Glittering with diamonds," said Sarah.

"Only one diamond," said Saffy.

"But very large," pointed out Sarah.

"So large," said Saffy, "it is hard to believe it is paid for. Unless it is just a biggish chunk of glass."

"It's real," said Rose. "I chose it! I went with Michael to buy it! And it's paid for. I saw him pay. So."

"So," agreed Caddy peacefully, and settled down for the holiday, spending her evenings working in a pub, and her days sunbathing in the garden.

"Sunbathing!" said Tom, looking up at the gray-and-white sky. He disapproved of the whole idea of sunbathing. He thought it was far too summery an occupation. A part of Tom was still denying that summer would ever come, and so far the English weather had been completely on his side.

"It *is* getting quite hot," said Indigo.

"Hot!" said Tom scornfully.

"It is though," said Rose. "We don't need coats anymore."

"You still carry them around all the time," pointed out Tom, and Indigo explained to him that in England, summer was when you carried your coat around instead of wearing it. Only for a few reckless days in August, said Indigo, could it be safely left at home.

"What a country!" said Tom, tossing his ball to Indigo. "Catch! Hey, you caught it! When are we going up that church tower? Saturday?"

"All right, Saturday," agreed Indigo, and on Saturday they went, taking Rose in her Permanent Rose T-shirt with them.

"Why *Permanent Rose*?" demanded Tom as they climbed the worn stone steps of the narrow spiral staircase that wound to the top of the tower.

"It's a joke," explained Indigo. "It's the name of a paint color," and he recounted to Tom the story of how Rose had been given her name when she was a very small, very ill, very impermanent-seeming baby.

"I had a hole in my heart," said Rose over her shoulder. "I had to have it sewed up. Didn't I, Indy?"

"Yep," said Indigo.

"I nearly died," said Rose proudly. "And when the hole was sewed up I got something else that I always forget the name of."

"Pneumonia," said Indigo. "Slow down a bit, Rose."

"And I nearly died again. I didn't start getting well for ages. Caddy and Saffron and Indigo made me. They took turns."

"Took turns to what?" asked Tom.

"Make me get better. They used to stare at me and say 'Getbettergetbettergetbetter.' All the time."

"Not all the time," said Indigo. "Just often. To remind you."

"You used to poke me."

"Only to check you were still alive."

"I know. I didn't mind."

"How old were you?" asked Tom.

"One."

"You can't really remember anything about it then."

"I can. I remember as easy as anything Indigo's face looking through the yellow bars saying 'Getbettergetbetter.'"

"What yellow bars?"

"Crib bars," said Rose, and Tom stopped suddenly, so that Indigo bumped into him from behind, and said, "Oh yes! Crib bars! I used to pull myself up and bite the top."

"See how far back you can remember," suggested Rose.

Tom paused for a while to think, and then said triumphantly, "I can remember my mother saying 'Walk to Mommy!' That must have been when she lived with us. She went to work at Yellowstone. Before I was even two."

"Gosh! Worse than horrible Daddy!" said Rose.

"I don't remember minding her going at all. She told me she had to look after the bears. She used to send me pictures of them that she'd drawn. Getting tucked up and having their sneakers put on and stuff like that."

"Poor you."

"No, no," said Tom, starting up the stairs again. "I was fine. It was much more peaceful when she'd gone. And she still sends me bear pictures sometimes!"

They reached the top after that and had to concentrate on not letting Rose hang too far over the parapet. Indigo was pleased to find he felt surprisingly all right. Not comfortable, but not terrible either.

"Don't look down," Tom advised. "Look outward. Look across. Look at that flat roof on top of the school! I bet no one has been up there for ages."

"How could anyone get up there?" asked Rose.

"Easy," said Tom. "Up that fire escape at the back and onto the kitchen roof. Across the kitchen roof and round to where the porches begin. Along the porch to the bottom of the glass sloping roof of the art building. It's not glass at the edges, it's tile and metal. I checked. Then up the sloping roof, keeping against the wall where it meets the main tower building. Then up the tower building from there. It's only one more floor, and there're climbing rungs all the way up. Must have been where a fire escape was before they built the art building alongside."

"You've got it all worked out!" said Indigo in astonishment.

"Been planning it for weeks," said Tom. "You coming with me, Indigo?"

"Maybe one day."

"What's the point of talking about one day?" asked Tom, his mood suddenly swinging from up to down, as it too often did. "This time in two more weeks, do you know where I'll be?"

Talking to Tom's father had not been a success. Tom's grandmother had tried first, and when she had failed Tom himself had made an attempt. He had been met with cold fury.

"In all the time you have been away," Tom's father had said, "you have not contacted us once. Not a call. Not a word. Not a birthday card to your sister. Nothing. Also we have had three letters of complaint sent from the school that generously agreed to accommodate you. You have been a major nuisance and learned nothing. And I have decided, during your long and peaceful absence, that you have been indulged for long enough, and IT IS TIME YOU CAME HOME AND STARTED BEHAVING YOUR-SELF."

"Where?" asked Rose. "Where will you be this time in two weeks more?"

"Flying home," said Tom.

Chapter Fourteen

FOR THE FIRST TIME SINCE HE STARTED SCHOOL, INDIGO WAS not looking forward to the end of term. He ought to have been, because this promised to be a good summer. Caddy had spent her first three weeks' wages on the remains of a car and was promising to drive anyone anywhere. Eve was planning trips to London ("Of course Daddy will be pleased!"). Derek had invited them to stay at his camp.

Indigo would have exchanged all this for the chance to keep his friend. He ached at the thought of Tom leaving, missing him in advance.

Rose was also desolate, but unlike Indigo, she did not try to conceal her feelings. With Rose, unhappiness always took the form of bad temper. She lashed out furiously at all attempts to cheer her up.

"But Rose," said her father, tactless as ever, "I understood that Tom was actually Indigo's friend more than yours! Let's talk about something happy!

What about Caddy's wedding? It does sound fun!"

"It wasn't meant to sound fun! Sarah said it would bankrupt you!" snapped Rose.

Caddy, Saffron, and Sarah also found themselves under attack at the smallest excuse. Tom and Indigo received the worst treatment of all; they could hardly speak to Rose without being snarled at. She suspected them (rightly) of being sorry for her.

Another week passed, and the final days of the term came closer. School was to finish on Wednesday. On Thursday Tom's father would be flying to England, and on Saturday he would take Tom home again. That was it. There was nothing to argue about, nothing to hope for, nothing that could change. Tom no longer spoke of his father, not the astronaut, nor the baseball player, nor the really old, hippy old, rock and roller. Not even the person who had looked after him so well that he hardly missed his mother when she drifted away to take care of the bears in Yellowstone National Park.

He and Indigo talked about other things. The gang and its red-haired leader.

"Try not to let them slaughter you," advised Tom.

"I have been trying," replied Indigo.

"I hadn't noticed."

"Well," said Indigo. "Notice now! Am I slaughtered?"

"Not yet," said Tom.

They discussed the black guitar. Tom had visited the music shop again and had been allowed to spend a long time undisturbed, playing in the dimly lit stockroom, among the dusty boxes and abandoned instruments waiting for repair.

"I know that as soon as I stop going in they'll put it in the window again," he said to Indigo.

"I'll keep visiting for you."

"I suppose you can try."

"I'll take Rose," said Indigo, as one might say, "I'll take the Marines," and Tom was forced to grin.

Another thing that Tom often mentioned in those last few days was his old idea of climbing the school. One afternoon he led Indigo around the building, pointing out the route.

"No, thanks," said Indigo.

"Come on, Indigo! We'll light a bonfire on the top!"

"No."

"All right. No bonfire. What's the matter, Indigo? Feeling blue?"

Indigo laughed.

"It would be a good place to think," said Tom.

"I'll remember," said Indigo. "If I ever need to think."

Tom bounced a ball to him, one of the bagful returned to him that morning. The Head had made a small ceremony of it.

"I hope you will come and see us again," he had said, looking at Tom down his nose. "Your visit has been an enlightening experience for us all . . . violent sometimes . . ."—he glanced at Jason—"but interesting. Your property . . . I am delighted to have the opportunity to return it in person."

Here he handed Tom a grubby carrier bag of confiscated balls as solemnly as if he were handing over an ancient and valuable heirloom of the school.

"You have broadened our outlook . . . ," he told Tom. (The red-haired gang leader sniggered and then yelped as he received a confiscated ball, hard and accurate, smack on his right ear.)

". . . Broadened our outlook," repeated the Head, watching benignly as Tom retrieved and pocketed the ball, "which is the fundamental aim of all good education. . . . Shall you keep in touch?"

"No, sir," said Tom.

"Mmm," said the Head disconsolately, and wandered out of the room, completely disregarding the indignation of the red-haired gang leader. None of the rabble seemed to want to tackle Tom either, armed as he was with a bag full of rubber missiles and immunity from retribution. For the same reason they also left Indigo alone. Nearly alone. The red-haired gang leader had caught up with him in the madhouse at the door.

"We know where you live, Casson," he hissed, and his eyes gleamed with malice. "Don't you forget! When he's gone home, we know where you live!" And he added, when he was a long way away, almost out of earshot, "You and your dirty little sister."

On the final Wednesday of term Rose's school was to close at the end of the morning. This always happened. The idea was that the younger children should all be safely home before the older ones, rowdy with end-of-term wildness, were let out onto the streets from their school nearby.

The morning followed its usual timetable: the end of year assembly, a final distribution of lost property, the photographs, and the signing of T-shirts for the people who were leaving that year. Rose was one of the last to go home; her signature was always in demand with both boys and girls. She was popular, although she did not know it. She drew a rose.

The end of the morning came, the last photographs were taken, and the last T-shirts signed. There were even a few last tears to be wiped away. And then the school was suddenly empty, and by lunchtime Rose was home.

She found her mother in her shed, painting with the help of a handful of green feathers and some blurry photographs, as lifelike a picture as she could manage of a long-dead parrot.

"What do you think, darling?" she asked when Rose appeared at the door.

"It's only got one leg," said Rose, peering at a photograph.

"I know. That's why I put him in profile."

"Is he dead?"

"Years ago."

"I thought so," said Rose, and looked critically at

the picture for a little while longer before asking, "What about lunch?"

Eve left the parrot and came at once, and in the house she made hot chocolate and peanut butter sandwiches, recognizing that Rose needed a lot of comforting these days. They ate together in friendly silence, admiring for the hundredth time Rose's magnificent work of art on the kitchen wall.

"Rose," began Eve, after a while, "I wanted to say to you . . . about Tom . . ."

"Was the parrot born with one leg?" interrupted Rose, very quickly, through a mouthful of sandwich.

"No, no. He had an accident. . . ."

"Well then, you should paint him with two. Like he was before the accident. I'm not talking about Tom. You should paint the parrot young. With two legs. I wish I had four hundred and fifty pounds."

"I wish I had too."

"Why? What would you do with it?"

"Give it to you," said Eve, sounding surprised that Rose needed to ask. "I suppose I could try the parrot with two legs. And if it doesn't work paint one of them out again."

Rose nodded.

"Coming to help me?"

"I'll come and look when you have finished."

"Perhaps you would keep me company, just to talk. I get bored out in that shed."

"You don't really."

"Let's abandon the parrot, Rose darling, and go and do something completely different! We could . . . we could . . . go to the supermarket and buy a feast for when everyone comes home!"

Rose was so touched by the heroism of this suggestion that she got up and put her arms round her mother's neck.

"Brilliant idea?" asked Eve, rocking her.

"No."

"Oh, Rose."

"I wish I could see the parrot with two legs."

"I'll do it right away," said Eve, and tried not to mind when Rose wriggled out of her arms.

When Eve had gone back to her shed, Rose went up to Indigo's bedroom. Tom's guitar lay on the bed in its case. Rose took it out, but she did not try to play it. She rested her cheek gently on its scratched wooden surface and stayed like that for a long time.

Then she sat up.

She turned the guitar over and looked at the crack in the back. To hear Tom talk about it you would think the whole guitar was about to fall into two halves, but to Rose's eyes the crack was very small—long, but hardly the width of a fingernail.

He should fill it up with glue, thought Rose.

In the kitchen drawer downstairs there was a treasure trove of mending stuff, all sorts of glue and tape and screwdrivers and things like that.

Rose went downstairs and began to rummage through it.

There was one sort of glue described on its label as stronger than nails. When Rose went back up to Indigo's room she took it with her, along with a tin of furniture polish, a duster, and the roll of tape Derek had once used to bind around the joint of a leaky faucet. Rose had watched him do it, and she had many times been shown the too-loose tuning pegs on Tom's guitar.

The furniture polish worked wonderfully, removing fingerprints and covering scratches. Rose cheered up immensely as she rubbed. She thought, *Tom could paint it black. I won't paint it black,* decided Rose virtuously, *but Tom could.*

Polishing the strings and fingerboard turned the cloth dark gray.

All that dirt off, thought Rose with satisfaction, and very much encouraged by her success she tackled the slipping tuning pegs. She intended to wind them round with tape, as Derek had wound the faucet joint. If it worked as she hoped, they would be tighter and stronger, and if it did not work, the tape could come off again with no harm done.

Each peg was shaped like a little screw which turned a cog that tightened or loosened the strings. Rose unscrewed and unscrewed and unscrewed. The strings got so loose they slipped off easily and flew free, twining around her arms and catching in her hair. She bundled them all together into the sound hole to be out of the way. Still the pegs did not come off. Rose inspected their fixings again and went for a screwdriver.

Very soon all six were free, and so were a lot of other things. Pegs and cogs and tiny screws, as well as the metal plates that held everything in place. Rose piled them all up in the middle of the bed and thought bravely, *I know where they all go back.*

"I know where they all go back," Rose said out loud, although she could hardly bear to look at them.

"I'll just do the gluing, and then I'll sort them out."

A cold feeling of fear was beginning to stir inside her, somewhere near her stomach.

"Nothing is broken," said Rose staunchly, ignoring it.

The back took an awful lot of glue and only after a while did Rose realize why. Instead of setting stronger than nails and filling the crack, it was trickling straight through. It was dripping into the inside of the guitar. Already it was all over the strings. It glued them to each other, and to everything else they touched. It stuck fluff and hairs onto the polished woodwork, and somehow it got on Indigo's quilt. Then it was on the heap of things that Rose dared not look at. It was everywhere.

Rose became terribly frightened and she began to cry.

Downstairs the telephone rang. Automatically Rose jumped up, because she was the one who always grabbed the phone. She ran down the stairs and picked it up and it was her father.

"Just checking in!" he began breezily.

Rose could not speak. She sobbed and sobbed into the telephone receiver. Far away in London she heard her father calling desperately, "Rose, what is it? What is the matter? Rose? TALK to me, Rose!"

"Daddy, Daddy!" wailed Rose.

"Rose! Are you hurt? Is someone hurt?"

"Something awful! I have done something awful!"

"Rose! Rose, are you on your own?"

"I have done something awful," sobbed Rose. "Awful, awful! Daddy, come home. Daddy, come home quick! I have done something awful!"

Indigo and Tom's school also finished earlier than usual that final Wednesday. They walked home together to Tom's grandmother's house without talking much. The sky was very blue and clear, so that the trails left by the jet planes lasted for ages, and the planes themselves were visible, like translucent blue arrows.

"It always seems so weird to think there are people inside," remarked Tom, looking up at one as it crossed the sky, "reading the newspapers and watching videos and having drinks. . . ." His voice trailed away, and Indigo did not answer.

There was trouble waiting for them at Tom's house. The first thing they saw when they went in was his grandmother, staring at the telephone as if it had just attacked her.

"What's the matter?" asked Tom, alarmed, and she

said, with no attempt to break the news gently, "You can't go home."

"I can't?" Tom looked at her in amazement. Then, as the news sank in, he repeated, with growing delight, "I can't go home?"

"No. Your father just telephoned. He's not coming."

"Fantastic!"

"Frannie is in the hospital. She's very ill. She's in intensive care. . . . Frances . . . Poor little Frances . . ."

"So how long can I stay?" interrupted Tom eagerly. "Tell me what he said!"

"She's very, very ill. She has meningitis, Tom. She's only a baby." Tom's grandmother turned abruptly away.

Tom looked across at Indigo in dismay and mouthed, "Crying?"

Indigo nodded.

Tom's usual method of dealing with stressful situations was to get as far away as he could and think about something else. If that was not possible he bounced a ball and thought about something else. This time, however, neither seemed appropriate. Awkwardly he patted his grandmother on the back and said, "Try not to worry, Gran!" He glanced at Indigo, raised his eyebrows, and jerked his head toward the door, heroically offering his friend the chance to escape.

Indigo shook his head.

Tom looked relieved and put a little more effort into his banging on his grandmother's back. It became more like drumming, quite fast and hard.

Indigo whispered, "Who is Frances?"

"Just some kid," muttered Tom, looking extremely shifty.

"What kid?"

Tom looked everywhere but at Indigo and muttered, "She's like, my father's kid . . . ," and the drumming turned into quite hard thumping. It seemed to bring his grandmother back to normal all at once, because she said, "Stop it, Tom!" quite sharply, and moved away.

Indigo, who was staring at Tom in complete astonishment, asked, "Your father's kid? Your *sister*?"

"Not really. Only half sister."

"Has Tom never told you about Frances?" demanded Tom's grandmother, looking at Indigo. "Has he never mentioned his sister at all?"

"Gran," asked Tom, returning to what seemed to him to be the most important aspect of the situation, "did Dad say anything about how long I could stay?"

"Tom!" almost shouted his grandmother. "Frances is in the hospital! She is dreadfully ill! I despair of you! *I despair of you!*"

There was a shocked silence while she and Tom stared at each other, mutually outraged.

Indigo took charge. There were a dozen things he did not understand, but he pushed them to one side.

"We'll make you some tea," he said to Tom's grandmother. "That will make you feel better. I think Tom just hasn't got it yet. About Frances. He's not meaning to be horrible. . . ."

"Me? Being horrible?" demanded Tom indignantly.

"He's just not thinking straight. Put the kettle on, Tom!"

"Put it on yourself!" said Tom angrily.

"He's in shock." Indigo filled the kettle. "Like I would be if it was Rose . . ."

At that moment, out of nowhere, the memory returned to Indigo of the red-haired gang leader taunting him the day before. He remembered the half-caught words he had heard: "You and your dirty little sister!"

"Like I would be if it was Rose," repeated Indigo.

All at once, he was worried about Rose. He had a sudden, uncanny feeling, that she was in trouble somewhere.

"Rose?" asked Tom.

Indigo glanced up and found that Tom was looking at him very oddly, as if he were trying to see right through his head.

"Indigo," said Tom, "Frances isn't like . . . it's not the same. . . . You care about . . ."

Tom stopped himself just in time, muttered, "I only said I thought you should try not to worry," to his grandmother, and disappeared out of the door.

She sat down and held her head in her hands.

"I think he is right," said Indigo, pulling himself together and beginning to make tea. "You should try not to worry. Babies are tough. Rose was in the hospital for weeks and weeks when she was a baby. I told Tom."

"You heard him," said Tom's grandmother bitterly. "He doesn't care."

"He does."

"I went to visit them a year ago, just after Frances was born. He wouldn't look at her."

"He's always really nice to Rose," said Indigo staunchly.

"He hated it when his father remarried."

"I suppose it was hard to get used to."

"He didn't try. He got worse, not better. That's why I had him over here. To give them all a breathing space. I thought he would come to his senses and be glad to go back, but he's been pleading to stay. . . . Well, he's got what he wanted now! I wish I knew where he had gone to."

"I'll go and look for him if you like."

"The trouble with Tom is he has been an only child for too long. He seems to need to be center stage. He loves an audience."

"Well, we like him like that," said Indigo, more than a little defensively. "I expect Frances will, too, when she gets better. He'll make her laugh, like he does Rose. And tell daft stories and play his guitar . . ."

Again the strange feeling came that Rose was in trouble, but just then the telephone rang, and Tom's grandmother jumped, spilling her tea.

"Will you go and find Tom?" she called to Indigo as she hurried to answer it. "You know where he goes to. . . . Please, Indigo?"

Indigo hesitated.

"Please." Her voice was quavery and tight. "He should be here. I need him to be here."

"I'll go right now," said Indigo.

Chapter Fifteen

she went back upstairs to Indigo's room. For a long time her mind was blank with dismay, and she sat completely numb, staring at the broken guitar.

Then, suddenly, like a light switched on, she thought of the music shop.

The music shop would be able to help.

Rose jumped to her feet and began feverishly gathering up the dismantled heap of pegs and cogs and screws. She bundled them up in her school sweatshirt, seized the guitar, ran down the stairs, out of the house, and along the road to town.

By this time every school in town was out for the holidays. The streets were teeming with students, silly with exuberance at the thought of summer. The townspeople glanced at the crowds discontentedly, and muttered the old familiar complaint that the holidays were far too long. Rose barged through them all as if they did not exist.

The town bridge had been taken over by the gang from Indigo's class. They were all there, red-haired leader, rabble, and hangers-on, eating french fries and pizza, throwing Coke cans into the river, exchanging loud and insolent comments on the passing public, and knocking each other about in a mild sort of way. People avoided them, but Rose did not. Across the bridge, on the opposite side of the road, was the turning that led to the music shop. Clutching her bundle and hugging the guitar close to her chest, Rose plunged right into the middle of the gang.

There seemed a great many of them to Rose, big boys, smelling of dusty clothes and pizza, bubble gum and sweat. Their voices were loud and alien. They blocked Rose's way and she kicked them. She knocked into somebody and he dropped his Coke can and swore. Rose, with her eyes fixed on the opposite side of the road, dodged and shoved and broke free and ran.

All at once she was grabbed from behind.

Two boys had hold of her arms and were pulling her backward. She fell sprawling and dropped the guitar. There was a horrible sound of cracking wood.

Then Rose was hauled to her feet again, the guitar

was snatched up by a third boy, and a van driver who had stopped on the bridge in the nick of time, restarted his engine, yelled at them one last time, and went on his way.

The boy who had picked up Tom's guitar looked at the dirt and splinters, the tangled gluey strings, and the spilled contents of Rose's bundle, pegs and cogs and screws scattered all over the pavement and gutter. He said, "Wrecked!"

Then Rose went crazy. She pulled herself free from her tormentors and kicked and lashed like a wild thing.

"It's that kid sister of Indigo Casson's," the red-haired gang leader said. "I warned him! Get her!"

Nobody got Rose. She got them instead, starting with the two who had pulled her back from under the wheels of the van. While they were still protesting, she attacked the one who had saved the guitar from being smashed entirely, and then, in her misery, she fought indiscriminately.

Indigo, hurrying through town in search of Tom, turned a corner and took it all in. It was everything he had ever feared: Rose, in the center of the gang, her face streaming with tears, the smashed guitar, and the seething rabble. He heard the red-haired gang leader call, "Drop it in the river!"

Then Indigo launched himself into battle. In the next few minutes he made up for all the fights he had not fought in the year that had passed, and Rose joined in.

The rabble, bruised and bleeding, behaved like heroes. They held the guitar out of harm's way when the battle raged closest. They fended Rose off from the edge of the curb, over and over again. When Indigo got the red-haired gang leader down on the ground and knelt on him, deaf to his tears and pleas for mercy, and looked like he was never going to stop hitting him, they pulled him off and held his arms behind his back until he calmed down enough to hear what they were saying.

"Crikey, Indigo! Slow down!"

"Let Tony get up now, Indigo!"

"Your sister's not safe to be let out! She would have run straight in front of a delivery van!"

"Look! She bit me!"

"We pulled her down, but nobody meant to hurt her. We had to."

"Let me go!" demanded Indigo, glaring at the red-haired boy, now sitting hunched against the wall of the bridge, and they tightened their grip and said, "Think Tony's had enough just now, Indigo!"

Then at last Indigo began to understand what had happened, and he looked across at the boy by the wall again.

"Is he all right?" he asked.

A couple of people pulled Tony up, dusted him down a little, and said, "Fine! Look! Indigo says are you all right, Tony? You're fine, aren't you?"

Tony staggered on his feet. His face was white, with crimson blotches. He stared around at the rabble, and then at Indigo. He could not seem to grasp that his days were over. He glanced toward Rose and said, "I told you to get her."

The rabble, his loyal rabble, whom he had guided and encouraged, coaxed and pushed for so long, looked at him as if he were almost a stranger.

Someone remarked casually, "Off his planet!" and there was a ripple of laughter.

Most people did not even bother to speak.

There was a feeling of lightness in the air, as if a storm had gathered and broken and left clear sky behind it. The rabble examined their wounds with a sort of pleasure. They felt like they had been under a cloud, and now it had blown away. This time they had not been the bullies. This time they had been attacked unfairly, and they had responded like stars.

Now the past was canceled. Justice had been done.

A small group, with Marcus as self-appointed expert, were examining the remains of the guitar. Others were collecting together the contents of Rose's bundle. Josh was showing her the circle of tooth marks she had left on his wrist.

The group was beginning to break up.

One rabble member was caught by his mother and was being forced to gather up all the french fry wrappers they had dropped in the street. Three hangers-on, who had been left out of all the action, were draped over the bridge parapet, trying to spit into the river.

The redheaded boy tried one last time. He looked at them all and spoke. He said, "Who's coming with me? I'm going."

He stood still and waited. Nobody took the slightest notice.

He took a step backward and then another.

"I'm going, I said."

"See you, Tone," said David kindly.

Meanwhile time was passing, and Indigo, back in his right mind and anxiously inquiring of everyone if he had hurt them, was torn between his promise to find Tom and the need to get Rose safely home. The state of the guitar was another huge problem. General opinion was that if it was taken to the music shop in its present condition, by Indigo or Rose in their present condition (filthy, tear-stained, bloodied, and penniless), they would be thrown out as soon as they got through the door.

"They'd probably ring the police," said Marcus. "They'd definitely ring your mother! Better go home and get cleaned up and find some money."

"Rose ought to be home, anyway," said Indigo worriedly. "And I promised Tom's grandmother I'd find Tom. She needs him; she's really upset. And now I've got to tell him his guitar is smashed."

Rose hiccuped and Marcus said hastily, "They'll be able to do something with it at the shop."

David said, "You go and find Tom, Indy. We'll see Rose home. Come on, Rose. Let's get you to your mother!"

Indigo looked at him uncertainly, longing to be off

looking for Tom. He asked, "That all right, Rose? You'll go with David and Marcus and Josh?"

Rose nodded.

"I'll carry the guitar," said Josh. "David has got all the pieces that came off."

"You'll see her right to the house?" asked Indigo. "Right to the house and inside? Look in the shed if it seems like there is no one about. My mother will be painting in there."

"Okay."

"Don't leave her on her own."

"'Course not."

When Rose said to her father. "I have done something awful! Daddy, come home!" it frightened him. He had panicked. Grabbed his bag. Locked his flat. Raced to the station and caught the first train home.

Marcus, Josh, and David, escorting Rose like a guard of honor, got to the house and found no one there. Eve had gone hunting for Rose only minutes before. However, she had left the back door open, in case anyone should return before she did. David took the guitar inside and propped it in a corner of the kitchen. Marcus and Josh, following Indigo's instructions, went with Rose to the shed. It, too, was empty.

"Indigo said not to leave her on her own," said Marcus. They were all hesitating by the back door, wondering what to do next, when a taxi pulled up in the street outside and Rose's father jumped out.

"Daddy!" shrieked Rose, and flung herself upon him.

Marcus, Josh, and David took one look at him, immaculate suede jacket, black shirt, designer hair-cut, and expression of absolute fury as he saw the state of Rose, and they disappeared like smoke blown in the wind.

Rose and her father took no notice. They hugged each other and shook each other, and shouted their opinion of each other's behavior, and when the worst was over Rose started wailing again that she had done something terrible.

"Rose," said her father. "You are eight years old! Nothing you could do can be that terrible!"

Rose wailed even louder.

"Rose!" shouted her father. (He had to shout because Rose's wailing was now at the hee-hawing, donkey-sounding stage.) "Come to the house and tell me what you think you have done. Whatever it is, I promise I will fix it!"

By this time they had reached the door that led in to the kitchen.

"Whatever it is," Bill assured Rose very tenderly as he led her inside.

He meant it. It shocked him to see Rose, brave, aggravating, self-assured Rose, in such a state of unhappiness.

"Whatever it is, whatever you have done, I will fix it," Bill promised, and Rose believed him and stopped crying.

Her father straightened up, and then for the first time ever, he saw Rose's picture on the kitchen wall. Rose had forgotten until that moment how much she had longed to show it to him, but now she watched him, and her heart was beating very fast, and her tears were all dry.

Bill Casson, usually so self-controlled, was staring with his mouth hanging open. The picture was so huge, so dominating, such a multitude of colors and complex images. He was shaken right through to think that such a thing could have been created in his absence.

Rose waited for him to speak.

Her father assumed he had discovered the source of her tears, the awful thing she had done, and he showed amazing restraint. He did not get angry. He swallowed back the words, "I told your mother not to take you to that damn silly graffiti class." Instead, he said very gently, with his arm around Rose, "Don't worry sweetheart, it will scrub off."

"Scrub off?" said Rose.

"Well, maybe not completely. But it will certainly paint over."

"Paint over?"

Rose looked at him, at first in disbelief, and then with growing understanding. There he was at last, loving her, worried about her, having rushed all the way from London to comfort her. Promising he would make everything all right. She loved him, and she hated him, all at the same time.

Still with his arm around her he tested a bit of the picture with his fingernail, one of the sharks conjured up by Rose to devour his uncaring carcass. He scratched right through the shark skin to the plaster underneath and said triumphantly, "There! Look, darling! I told you it would scrub off! Was Mummy very cross?"

Rose was speechless.

Her father still did not get angry. He was not angry. His intention was what it had always been, to save the situation, rescue Rose, and sort out whatever terrible thing she had done, at whatever the cost to himself. So he sat down, pulled Rose onto his lap, and said bravely, "You and I could get that cleaned away in no time at all!"

It was impossible to tell from his voice that he did not really believe this for a moment, and actually thought it would take several days of backbreaking, hand-ruining scraping.

"That's not the terrible thing I did," said Rose.

"I'll have to go into town and buy some jeans and a T-shirt or two to work in. . . ."

"I did something much worse than that!"

". . . There's an appointment or two, several actually, I'll need to cancel in London. . . ."

Rose slid off his knee, crossed the kitchen, picked up Tom's guitar, shoved it under her father's nose and said, "*This* is the terrible thing!"

"What!"

"It's Tom's guitar. I tried to mend it and I made it much worse. And I fell down on it and made a big crack. And some of the bits I unscrewed got lost and one of the pegs is all bent. A van ran over it."

"That's the terrible thing?" asked Bill, astonished.

"Yes."

"What you were so miserable about?"

"Yes."

"But surely," said Bill, completely bemused, "it can be replaced, Rose sweetheart!"

"What?"

"Isn't one guitar as good as another? More or less? I would have thought so!"

He was so immensely relieved to find Rose safe and well, and nothing worse to deal with than a broken guitar, that he stretched up his arms and laughed. Then he sat back and sighed with relief and suddenly remembered something he had grabbed just before he left his London studio. A picture, to show to Rose.

He leaned sideways, pulled his bag toward him and took it out.

Rose's heart sank.

Inside was a portrait, not quite finished, done in ink and watercolor washes. It was painted from the photograph Caddy had seen in her father's studio. Rose in her glasses. Truculent. Bewildered. Rose, lost among reflected Roses, at least a dozen of them, fading forward and backward like a dream.

"What do you think?" asked Bill.

Very unwillingly, Rose looked, and she was astonished. She said, "It's me!"

"Yes."

"It's good." She gulped back a sob, but said again, because it was true, "It's really good." Then she looked at the broken guitar and began to cry once more.

"Can't we just buy Tom a new one?" asked her father, who at that moment of triumph would have bought anybody anything.

"They cost a lot of money," said Rose.

"You expect to have to pay if you want quality," said Bill calmly. "Isn't there a music shop in town somewhere?"

"Yes," said Rose, hardly able to believe her ears, "and there's a guitar in it that Tom has been wanting for weeks and weeks and weeks. Can we go right now?"

Bill said magnificently that of course they could go right now, and he allowed himself to be towed into town straightaway. And if he regretted his magnificence a little when he saw the price of the black guitar, he did not allow Rose to know. After all, she had liked his picture. And he was used to spending money, far better at it than Eve would ever be. Also, the shop assistant helped very much, recognizing Rose at once, and congratulating her father on being such a discerning and generous purchaser.

"Of course it's for your friend?" he asked Rose.

"Tom," said Rose.

"Tom. Of course. Give him my good wishes, won't you."

"Yes, I will," said Rose.

Then she and her father walked home together, Bill striding along as if he owned the town, Rose hopping and skipping beside him, as temporarily happy as she had ever been in her life.

"I loved your letters," said Bill.

"Did you?"

"Made me laugh out loud."

"They weren't meant to make you laugh."

"Oh. What were they meant to do?"

"Make you come home," said Rose.

It had been hours since Indigo set out to look for Tom. There was nowhere he had not searched: backward and forward to Tom's home and his own, all through town, to the music shop, the library, the church tower, even the multistory car park.

Indigo had climbed them all.

Evening arrived before he realized where Tom must be.

Although he had been half expecting him all afternoon, it startled Tom considerably when, glancing toward the west where the sun was setting, a hand appeared clutching the rail at the top of the fire escape.

Then the top of a head. Windblown, lanky brown hair.

("Much too long," Saffron always said. "Let me and Sarah cut it!" "No!")

Then the other hand stretched up, and Tom was ready for that one, and he reached out and pulled Indigo over the parapet and hugged him.

"Go on then, say it," said Indigo.

Tom grinned and asked, "Feeling blue, Indigo?"

"Not particularly."

The top of the school was covered in a sort of gravel, dark and mossy with age. Indigo stretched out flat on his back. The climb had taken less than ten minutes, but it felt like hours.

He said, "Hey, Tom, the sky's going green."

"I've been worrying about that," said Tom, also flat on his back, and they looked at it together. There was not a cloud nor a plane nor a bird. Just the blue-green clearness of a summer evening.

"I brought a bag of cherries," remarked Indigo, fishing in his pocket.

"You think of everything," said Tom. "Do you know what I found up here? A little tree. It's growing over there by the wall. There's been a pigeon too."

"Spit out your cherry stones as far as you can," said Indigo. "We'll have an orchard up here in no time."

"We need never go down, once the cherries are ripe."

"No."

"Sky's getting greener all the time. There'll be stars next if we're not careful."

"Probably," agreed Indigo philosophically.

"Indigo?"

"Mmmm?"

"You wouldn't run down for my guitar?"

"Couldn't you just hum?"

"Not really."

"I've got an awful lot of stuff to tell you."

"I've got to go home."

"I know."

"You'd go home if Frances was Rose and you were me, wouldn't you?"

"Yes."

"What if she dies, and I've just been horrible to her all her life?"

"Your grandmother telephoned the hospital again this afternoon. They said she'd stabilized."

"What's that mean?"

"It's good. She's not getting worse."

"I've got a proper chance then."

"'Course you have."

"What was that you used to say to Rose?"

"Getbettergetbettergetbetter."

"I'll do that then. On Saturday."

Indigo thought of something. "Your dad can't come. Will they let you fly on your own?"

"I did before, to come here."

"Oh yes," said Indigo unhappily.

Tom said, to comfort them both, "It's not that far. It's just through a patch of that."

"What?"

"Sky."

"Quite a big patch," said Indigo.

"I know. But it's not like there's anything in between. It's not like you have to climb over walls. Or hack through jungle. Or swim."

"You could swim."

"Indigo," said Tom. "Be reasonable. You couldn't. Don't go trying."

"All right."

"There's a star. I told you it would happen. You know all that stuff I used to tell you. About my dad being an astronaut? And a baseball player? And my mother and the bears? All that stuff?"

"Yep."

"'Sall true."

They both laughed.

"Listen," said Indigo. "I'm going to tell you something terrible. Rose tried to mend your guitar."

"She did?" demanded Tom, sitting up very quickly.

"She took off all the strings and she unscrewed the tuning pegs."

Tom wrapped his arms around his head and moaned at the sky.

"She glued up the crack in the back with super-glue and then she took it into town. On the way she fell down and cracked it quite badly."

"She did what?" howled Tom.

"Then she panicked and fetched my dad from London to help."

"I thought he never came home."

"He does in emergencies. He bought you the black guitar."

"What?"

"He bought you the black guitar."

"Your father bought me the black guitar?"

"Yes. Let go of my throat."

Tom flopped down on the roof and lay limply staring upward.

"I beat up Tony Albinoni this afternoon," said Indigo.

"You beat up Tony Albinoni?"

"Yes."

"Why?"

"What do you mean, why?"

"What's he ever done to you?" asked Tom, and then laughed until he was nearly ill.

Chapter Sixteen

THE CASSON HOUSE WAS FULL OF PEOPLE. CADDY AND Michael. Saffron and Sarah. Also Derek, who, unaware of any crisis, had turned up quite by chance because Eve had mentioned on the phone that the kitchen sink was once again refusing to drain.

"I came as soon as I could," Derek announced as he pushed open the door (without knocking), pulled off his motorcycle helmet, and creaked into the kitchen.

Derek was dressed, as always, head to toe in muddy black leather. He kissed Eve, tripped over Sarah's wheelchair, spotted Bill, and said, "Hello! Visitors! Introduce me, Rose!"

"This is Daddy," said Rose obligingly. "Daddy, this is Derek, Caddy's old boyfriend. Mummy's having him now."

Rose stepped back to observe the results of this announcement. Her father, she anticipated, would immediately pull off his jacket and challenge Derek to a duel on the lawn. The winner (maybe Derek, clad as he was in black leather armor; perhaps Bill, who had the double advantages of unimpeded movement and a very thick skin) would claim Eve for his own. Thus would all confusion about who belonged to whom be fairly and finally settled.

Rose was very disappointed by what followed.

"Ah yes," said Bill, shaking hands perfectly calmly. "Yes, Derek. Very nice to meet you at last. Eve has talked of you. You must both come up to London and meet my . . . er . . . my . . . er . . . my . . . er . . . Samantha!"

Eve heaved a sigh of relief. Caddy and Michael gave each other hugely significant looks. Sarah and Saffron, who had winkled the secret out of Caddy weeks before, snorted with laughter.

Derek and Bill ignored them all and talked about drains and wiring so boringly that Eve stopped looking relieved and began to look slightly hunted—like a person who, having escaped the frying pan, is beginning to suspect they have landed, for all their leaping, into the fire.

"I wish Indigo and Tom would come home," said

Rose, for about the tenth time that afternoon. "I know where they are. I wish they'd come down."

Gradually, as the light faded and evening came, people began to realize just how long the boys had been missing. Derek and Bill, out in the shed admiring the new wiring, looked at their watches more and more frequently. Tom's grandmother telephoned again and again.

Eve said, "They're just taking a little time out together," and tried not to look out of the window every minute or so to see if they were on their way. Caddy and Michael drove around the streets in search of them but came back unsuccessful. Saffron and Sarah said, "Listen to Rose."

Rose said, as she had been saying for hours, that Tom and Indigo would undoubtedly be found on the top of the school tower building.

"But Rose *darling*," said Eve. "Why would they be up there?"

"To think," said Rose.

It was a while before anyone except Saffron and Sarah could be induced to take this theory seriously. Michael was the first to believe it might be possible. He said, "I suppose we do know they are that daft!"

"That's true," admitted Derek, and suggested that he and Michael, both experienced climbers, should take a quick look at the top of the school themselves, just to check.

This was done, after a little arguing with Bill. Derek and Michael drove over to the empty school, walked appraisingly around it once, said, "No problem at all!" and began to climb, following the exact route Tom had described, starting at the fire escape.

Sure enough, Rose was proved to be right. Tom and Indigo were discovered, perfectly safe, lying on their backs, renaming the stars. They pretended not to notice anything was happening until Derek emerged onto the roof and said kindly, "Come on, you two dreamers! Back down to planet Earth."

Tom sighed. Indigo asked, "How'd you know we were here?"

"Rosy Pose," said Michael, flopping down beside them. "Don't you fancy planet Earth then, Tom?"

"Not much," said Tom.

"Come on, Indy, time to go," urged Derek. "Before your dad calls out the troops. He wanted to ring the police and the fire brigade. We've left Caddy and Saffron and Sarah back home sitting on his head."

"Really sitting on his head?" asked Tom, brightening a little.

"Metaphorically sitting on his head," said Derek.

"What's Rose doing?"

"To be honest," said Derek, "I think she's not too happy. Let's get going."

Indigo and Tom came without any more protest. They had known from the moment they saw car headlights in the deserted school car park that their time of peace was over.

"You feeling blue yet?" Tom asked Indigo.

"Getting that way."

Derek organized their descent, first Michael, then Tom, then himself, and last of all, Indigo. He was a little worried about Indigo, but he need not have been. Indigo, who had been up and down every high building in the town that afternoon, managed perfectly easily.

From the moment they touched ground in the school car park time went so quickly it seemed to Tom and Indigo that they could feel the world spinning beneath their feet.

Negotiations, explanations, and arrangements

took over. Tom, stumbling through his grandmother's front door at midnight, said, "I've been thinking. I think I ought to get home quick."

"I think so too," his grandmother said. "The sooner the better. Middle of the night here is only early evening in America. I'll call your father at once."

"I'll do it," said Tom.

He did this straightaway, and the line went silent for so long that he was alarmed and asked, "Don't you want me to come home?"

His father sounded strange, far away and creaky. He said, "A few hours ago I thought I'd lost you both." He paused and then shouted, "*Of course* we want you to come home!"

After that his voice became normal again, and he and Tom suddenly found that they could talk to each other as they had not done for years and years. Their easy understanding came back as if it had never gone away. Tom told his father about Rose and Indigo, and about Rose's wonderful picture and Indigo's battle on the bridge. He told how Indigo had hunted through the town and climbed the school to find him. In loving detail he described the black guitar, which had not left his sight since Rose had pushed it into his arms. The fact that it was now his was still almost unbelievable to Tom.

"Do you think it will be all right on the plane?" he asked.

"Cover it with labels. Not just one. Put several on. And write our telephone number on them."

"How's Frances?"

"Hanging on."

Ten minutes after Tom put the phone down it rang once more, and it was his father again.

"Put a couple of labels on the inside of the case as well."

"Okay."

"And Tom, I've insured it. Your new guitar. Just in case. Tell Rose."

"I will."

"I'm going to try and get you an earlier flight. For tomorrow if I can manage it."

"Is Frances really that ill?" asked Tom, and his father said at once, "No, no, no, not at all! She is fine!"

This was so obviously untrue that Tom could think of nothing to say, and when his grandmother ordered "Bed," and took the telephone receiver from him, he did not try to argue. He picked up his guitar and climbed the stairs very slowly, too tired to think.

Bill Casson went back to London the next morning, but before he left he had a talk with Rose.

"What happened, Rose, when you said, 'Daddy come home'?"

"You came home."

"That will always happen."

"What if I say come home and horrible Samantha says stay?"

"She never would. And she's not horrible. You will meet her when you come to visit me."

"Can she cook?"

"What?"

"Can she cook?"

"Well, you know, Rose, being able to cook isn't everything!"

"I just thought if she was a nice fat strong lady who cooked all the time, like Sarah's mother, she might be useful."

Rose's father, sounding a little depressed, had to admit that Samantha was in no way like this description. Rose hugged him and said she would come to visit anyway. All her anger toward her father had gone. He would never really understand her. He still talked of the possibility of scrubbing her picture off the kitchen wall. He had drifted away from them all into another life, with hardly a backward glance. Still, he had come home when she asked him to, and he had bought Tom the black guitar. He was good and he was bad.

"Everyone is," said Derek, who had vanished the night before but reappeared again as soon as Bill was out of the house. "I see he didn't unblock the sink before he left."

"He's not the sink unblocking type," said Saffron.

"Lucky some of us are. How's Tom's sister this morning? Heard anything?"

"They're trying a new antibiotic. It hasn't had time to work yet."

"Fingers crossed then."

"They've got him an earlier flight. For tonight. Just in case . . . But Tom's father says she's a tough guy."

"That's good."

"What'll we do when he's gone?" asked Rose.

"Telephone," replied Derek as he tenderly

unscrewed the U bend of the kitchen sink. "Telephone, write, e-mail (don't tell me you haven't got a computer because I bet Sarah has!), take photos, draw pictures, learn to play guitar, save up your pennies for airplane tickets . . . Look at this drainpipe! Full of rock-hard oil paint! Has your lovely mum got no sense at all?"

"Nope."

"Chunks of the stuff!" continued Derek, knocking out lumps of rainbow-colored gunk into the kitchen trash can. "I've got to go in a minute, but before I do I wanted to tell you something, Indigo. I've got a friend who owes me a favor who has a friend who owes him a favour who says he can put that old Spanish guitar back together. I was talking to them both last night. Said he could put on a new back and restring it, no problem at all. How about that?"

"I think that would be brilliant," said Indigo, gratefully. "Thanks, Derek. I'll tell Tom when he gets here. He's coming round as soon as he can to say good-bye."

Tom, when he arrived to say good-bye, was very pleased to hear of Derek's suggestion.

"It seemed awful to think of throwing it away," he said.

"When it's fixed, can Indy have it?" asked Rose.

"He can borrow it," said Tom, and spent the next hour writing out chord patterns and finger exercises for Indigo, watching carefully as he tried them out on the black guitar.

"Your left hand fingers wave about too much," he said critically. "You want to keep them much closer to the strings. Rose, you'll have to watch his left hand!"

"I will," promised Rose.

"Tom, how much time have you got?" asked Caddy suddenly, and Tom looked at his watch and realized that he had no time at all. Working with Indigo he had been so engrossed that he had forgotten he had only come over to tell them good-bye. Rose saw his face as he struggled to find words he did not want to say and she did not want to hear. Sliding past Caddy, completely unobserved, she disappeared from the room.

Saffron and Sarah helped Tom begin his hard task, hugging him extravagantly, saying, "Promise to ring the second you get back! Wiggle your eyebrows one more time! What a pity you never let us cut your hair! Wave to us out the plane window as you fly over! Look, he's laughing! He's glad to go!"

Tom, smiling despite himself, was pounced on next by Eve.

"Bye-bye, Tom darling," she said, kissing him quickly. "I hope everything is all right forever and ever! Oh dear! I'm sorry! Take no notice of me!"

Eve rushed outside to cry in the shed.

"Good-bye, Caddy."

"Take care, Tom. We are going to miss you so much! I'll bring Indy and Rose across to see you one day, I promise."

"Where is Rose?" asked Tom, looking around.

Rose had vanished. Caddy went to hunt for her and returned after a while saying she was nowhere to be found. This was not true. Rose was under Caddy's bed, pressed as close as she could get to the wall. The sound of sniffling gave her away. Caddy bent down and peered underneath and found herself looking straight into Rose's defiant eyes.

"I'm busy," Rose had growled, and Caddy had nodded understandingly and tiptoed away.

"Tell Rose good-bye from me," said Tom unhappily. "Indigo . . ."

"I'll walk back with you," said Indigo quickly. Now that the time had come, now that there was no time at all, Indigo could not take in that Tom was truly going. This day. This afternoon. Now. It was unbelievable.

He and Tom walked back together, not talking much. Tom's grandmother had the car all loaded, ready for the journey to the airport. She said hello to Indigo and climbed into the driver's seat, tactfully allowing them a little peace.

Tom said, "Don't forget to say good-bye to Rose for me."

"I won't."

"If you only borrow my old guitar, then one day you'll have to give it back. That's why I said borrow. I wasn't being mean."

"I know."

"Bye then, Indigo."

"Bye, Tom."

Tom got into the car and rolled the window down. His grandmother started the engine. They both called something to Indigo, but he could not quite hear what it was. Perhaps they waved, but he did not see them do it. He could hardly make out the shape of the car as it drove away.

Afterward he walked the streets like a person in a dream. His feet took him into town, but his mind took him nowhere. He felt as alone as if he had stepped out of time. He felt invisible again.

He did not know how far he had walked, but somewhere along the way David fell into step beside him. By the time Indigo noticed him, David, always a round and breathless sort of boy, was panting and red-faced with the effort to keep up. Indigo dimly recognized this and slowed his pace a little.

David said brightly, "Hi, Indigo."

"Hello."

"I could see you hadn't noticed me. I just thought I'd ask, you around this summer?"

"Yes. Yes, I suppose so."

"I thought perhaps we could go bowling one day."

"That would be good."

"Maybe to the skateboard park?"

"Yes. Good idea."

"Think Tom would come too?"

"Oh yes," said Indigo, and then pulled himself

together and said, "No. He's gone back to America."

"That's a shame."

"Mmmm."

"You'll miss him."

"Yep."

"Me too. I liked hearing him talk. All that stuff about his dad and the bears and that. I knew it wasn't true, but I liked hearing it."

Indigo grinned a little.

"I can't talk like that. I'm pretty boring, compared."

"Who's comparing?"

"Shall I ring you, then, about going bowling?"

"Yes. Thanks, David. I'll come."

David disappeared from Indigo's side, and he walked on alone, much more slowly now. Slower than David's pace. Slower than Rose trailing home from school. He was terribly, achingly tired.

"I'm only tired," he said, plodding through the kitchen door into Caddy's hug.

At home the complete Casson comfort machine was in full swing. Rose was out from under the bed, lured by Sarah with an enormous new sketch pad.

Now she was drawing something that she kept well hidden in the circle of her arms.

"Don't look!" she ordered Indigo.

"I won't," he said meekly.

Eve was cooking.

"Chicken soup," she said proudly. "Full of goodness! You've been gone for hours, Indigo darling! Make him a cup of tea, Saffy, and take his shoes off. I can't. Every time I stop stirring this soup it erupts like a volcano!"

"He can take off his own shoes," said Saffy. "But I'll get him some tea. Where's the big atlas? Sarah needs it."

Sarah was hanging over a very small world map in the back of someone's old diary.

"I know flying would be quicker," she told Indigo cheerfully. "I *will* work on flying! But just for now I've found an overland route!"

"Overland to where?"

"America, of course. By Europe and Asia. Perfectly simple. I'm a tiny bit worried about the Bering Sea, but I bet there's a ferry. Don't turn your nose up like that, Indy! It's just a matter of getting my parents across to France with the car, and then getting them totally lost."

"Sarah, darling!" said Eve.

"They *like* going to France," said Sarah, patiently. "And once they are there, it's land all the way. More or less. The thing to do is keep on heading East."

"And avoiding war zones," said Saffron.

"And *of course* avoiding war zones. All the way to the Bering Sea. Then you just pop down through Alaska and Canada, and across."

Rose sighed deeply into her sketch pad and said, "Mountains."

"Mountains!" repeated Sarah scornfully, turning pages in the big atlas that Saffron had now found for her. "Look! Here we are! This is where we'll start, and over there is where we're heading. Hardly any mountains!"

"Look again!" said Saffron. "Those bits they've colored in purple and icy blue? With black pointy tops? Like this one. Fourteen thousand and ninety-seven feet!"

"Well, the Alps perhaps," admitted Sarah. "And those in the middle. The Urals (horrible name). And I suppose the Rockies, but there's bound to be roads."

By supper time, she had found ways over, or under, or around, all obstructing mountains. An hour later, a foolproof method of getting her parents to begin the journey: "Get them drunk on cheap French wine. Bribe a local to give them wrong directions and then, when they've gone so far they can't turn back, tell them it's educational!"

"It's possible," admitted Saffron at this point. "Educational might just swing it!"

Outside it became properly dark. The family abandoned the kitchen to the chaotic results of Eve's soup making and moved into the sitting-room. Sarah and Saffron lay down on the carpet with the atlas between them and began checking out Russian ferry ports. Soon Caddy and Eve had joined in the game and were crossing continents with almost equal enthusiasm.

Rose was curled quietly in a corner of the sofa, dreaming over her sketch pad. Whatever she had drawn there was still unrevealed. Her family carefully turned their eyes away from it, knowing that in time it would be produced for their inspection, to puzzle or astonish them.

"Lend me your pencil, Rosy Pose?" begged Sarah from the floor.

Rose passed it down, and Sarah took it and drew

a firm black line from Russia to Alaska across the Bering Sea. She regarded it with great pleasure for a little while and then said, "Now we can get on."

"Alaska," said Caddy, peering over Sarah's shoulder. "There'll be gorgeous bears."

"Do you mind if we take a little time on the way to go gorgeous bear watching, Indy?" Sarah asked.

"Not at all," said Indigo, glancing at his watch.

All evening he had been very aware of the passing of time. At ten o'clock he looked at his watch again. Tom's flight would be just about to take off.

Indigo looked out of the uncurtained window into the dark, starry night. He thought of the planes he saw every day, heading west across the sky. Some of them really must be on their way to America.

Rose had slipped quietly out of the room. Indigo, silently doing the same, saw her hunting about in the kitchen cupboard, pushing aside pots of jam. A minute later she stole out of the house and into the garden.

Indigo followed, closing the door quietly behind him.

"Rose?" he called in a low voice, not wanting to startle her.

"I'm here," said Rose, and Indigo located her,

looking very small, flat on her back on the lawn. She had her glasses on.

"I'm looking at the stars," she said as he stretched out beside her. "These glasses are very good for stars. I can see them everywhere. Hundreds. How many are there, do you think?"

"Thousands and thousands."

"The ones that move are airplanes. One of them might be Tom's."

"Yes."

"I didn't used to know . . ." Rose stopped and swallowed, and then bravely began again. "I didn't used to know they were there. The stars. But now I can see them all. Plain as plain. Can you?"

Indigo suddenly found that he couldn't. To him the stars were just splashes of silver, blurring and fragmenting and dissolving in the sky.

"Frances will be all right when he gets there," said Rose.

"Yes. I'm sure she will."

"Do you think Tom's all right, too, Indy?"

"Well," said Indigo. "I suppose . . . I expect . . . he's a bit sad right now. Like us . . . But he'll be all right."

"Do you remember when I first got my glasses and saw the stars? And you said, 'Wish on the moving ones.'"

"Yes."

"You said it worked for airplanes, too."

"Yes."

Rose did not say any more, but she and Indigo stayed out for a long, long time, wishing, and watching the stars, the steady ones and the ones that passed with red and green lights across the sky.

Need more Rose in your life? Keep reading!

★ "Wonderful."
—*Kirkus Reviews*, starred review

permanent rose

By the award-winning author of SAFFY'S ANGEL and INDIGO'S STAR

HILARY McKAY

From Margaret K. McElderry Books
KIDS.SimonandSchuster.com

Chapter One

DAVID TRAMPED ALONG THE ROAD TO THE CASSON HOUSE trying not to think too far ahead. In his pocket was a packet of banana-flavored chews. He had started his journey with three packets (watermelon, lime, and banana), but now only banana was left. Every few steps he unwrapped a fresh sweet and bundled it into his mouth. He did the unwrapping in his pocket and the bundling in one quick furtive movement that looked like a yawn.

It was the last week of the school summer holidays, late August, and smotheringly hot. David was on his way to visit Indigo Casson, something he had been meaning to do all summer. The nearer he got to Indigo's house, the harder he chewed.

Chomp, chomp, chomp, went David, and then he accidentally gulped and swallowed before he had the next sweet unwrapped. For the first time since he had started out, his mouth was empty. Chewing had been David's way of stopping himself from thinking very hard. Now (and without any encouragement at all from David) his brain lurched into action.

What if Indigo's dad opens the door?

Please not him! prayed David as he fumbled with a particularly tight chew wrapper.

Indigo's father was an artist: Bill Casson. Artist.

It was hard to believe. He looked like someone from a TV ad for something very expensive. Sports cars. Or first class train travel. He did not look as if he had ever been near anything as messy as paint.

Two things about Indigo's father had alarmed David when they had met. The first was this inhuman cleanness. The second was the way he had glanced at David. As if David was someone he intended (for obvious reasons) to have nothing at all to do with. David, always aware of his lifetime's collection of guilty secrets struggling to escape, had been shocked at being seen through so quickly.

But Indigo's dad will be in London, David told himself, as he finally got the chew wrapper free at last. *He nearly always is in London.* David bit down comfortingly into a new sweet. *Good.*

Banana-flavored chews were the best. Watermelon were a little too exotic, and lime slightly sour. Banana were perfect. Except for being much too small. In a David-perfect world they would have been the size and shape of a smallish egg. And not wrapped.

I hope I don't see Indigo's mum, either, thought David, swallowing a chew whole to see if it hurt.

David did not actually know Indigo's mother; he did not know anyone's mother except his own. However, he assumed all mothers were more or less the same, and when he had stopped choking (it hurt), he loaded in a fresh new chew and made a plan.

If Indigo's mum answers the door, I'll run off!

The packet of sweets was no longer a packet. It was a stump submerged in wrappers. David absentmindedly scooped them out of his pocket as he trudged along and then suddenly turned back and began to scrabble them up again. Very recently (that day in fact) he had stopped being the sort of person who drops rubbish in the street. Now he was the sort of person who picks it up, and he was surprised at how different that felt. Extraordinarily noble, and embarrassingly grubby at the same time.

He kept a wary eye on Indigo's house as he collected his papers. An awful lot of girls lived there.

"How many sisters have you got?" he had once asked Indigo.

"Three," Indigo had replied, and then, reconsidering, "No, two really."

"Don't you know?"

Indigo said of course he knew, and he listed his sisters for David.

"Caddy. She's at college in London, but she's home for the summer."

"She's grown-up then," pronounced David. He did not like grown-ups. "Grown-up!" he repeated disconsolately.

Indigo said he supposed so. Caddy, scatty, golden-haired, last seen tearfully designing a gravestone for her most recent dead hamster, did not seem particularly grown-up.

"Caddy's the eldest," Indigo told David. "Then there's Saffron, but she's not really my sister; she's my cousin. She came to live with us ages ago when she was little, when her mother died. Her mother was my mother's sister, so we adopted her. Anyway, you know Saffron!"

David winced at the thought of Saffron, whom he knew only too well. She was fifteen, more than a year older than he and Indigo, clever, gorgeous, and ruthless. She and her best friend had once invaded the boys' washroom and attacked the leader of the most vicious gang in the school. Her friend had guarded the door to stop anyone from escaping while Saffron had nearly pulled off the gang leader's head. Not one of his henchmen, including David, had dared raise a finger to stop her.

What if Saffron opened the door?

David unwrapped the whole of the rest of the packet of chews and pushed them into his mouth all together. They fitted easily. Only two tiny yellow triangles of dribble at the corners of his lips showed that they were there at all.

Saffron'll have forgotten about me by now, thought David, who was a hopeful person.

The last of Indigo's sisters was very young, not quite nine, dark-haired and white-faced, completely different from Caddy and Saffron. Nothing about her was alarmingly good-looking, or grown-up, or tough. Her name was Rose. Permanent Rose.

• • •

"Permanent Rose!" said people whenever they heard Rose's name for the first time. "What kind of name is Permanent Rose?"

"It's my kind of name," said Rose.

"Is it a joke?"

That was the question everyone asked.

Everyone.

Even Rose's own father had asked it once.

Rose could just remember the huge indignant fuss he had made when she was four years old and her father had finally discovered that her amusing pet name was not, as he had always supposed, an amusing pet name at all.

"Permanent Rose!" he had repeated over and over again. "*Permanent Rose!* No!"

He had been filling in a form for a new passport, putting on all the children's names, so that they could travel with him. "Just in case," said Bill, who always did things just in case. Caddy, Saffron, and Indigo were already safely listed, and then he came to Rose. She was hanging around watching every move he made, the way she always did when he was home.

"Your turn, Rosy Pose!" he had said, smiling down at her.

Then he picked up Rose's birth certificate, which he had never happened to see before. And there it was.

Permanent Rose.

"Eve, *darling*!" said Bill (Eve was Rose's mother). *"Darling!"* repeated Bill (very indignant and far from amused). "What *were* you thinking of?"

Eve, who was also an artist, had been thinking of the color that painters use: permanent rose. A clear, warm color that glows with its own lively brightness, no matter how thinly spread. A color that does not fade. There had been a permanent rose–colored sky on the morning that Rose was born.

Rose had arrived into the world a lot earlier than anyone had expected her to do, and from the absolute beginning she had seemed very unthrilled about the prospect of having to stay. She had been like a visitor who hovers on a doorstep, wondering if it is worth the bother of actually coming in. People had sent flowers to Eve, but not baby toys or little clothes. It did not seem that Rose intended to be around long enough to need such things.

Eve knew quite well why she only got flowers. That was why one afternoon she had slipped out of the hospital and gone all by herself across the town to register the latest Casson's defiant name. Permanent Rose.

"Permanent Rose," said Tom, "is the coolest name on the planet!"

That had been back in the spring, when Tom had first arrived into Rose's life. He was an American boy, the same age as Indigo, who had spent the spring term at Indigo's school. Tom and Indigo and Rose had become best friends. It had not seemed to matter that Rose was only eight years old.

"More than eight," said Rose. "Nearly nine."

"Darling Rose, even nearly-nine-year-olds don't fall in love," said forgetful Caddy.

Caddy tried very hard to comfort Rose when Tom went away. It was not an easy job. It was like trying to comfort a small, unhappy tiger.

"Who said anything about falling in love?" growled Rose crossly. "Falling! Falling is by accident! I didn't fall in anything!"

"Oh. Right. Sorry, Rose."

"And I am *definitely* not in love!"

"No. Okay, Rosy Pose. Sorry about that, too."

Rose, who was sitting on Caddy's bed, hunched her knees up under her chin, turned her back, and sighed. Caddy sighed too. The room became very quiet until Rose asked suddenly, "What is the name for it when you are trying to paint a picture and you haven't any red? Or blue? Or yellow? When you finish a jigsaw and a piece is not there? When Indigo's guitar loses a string and a whole lot of notes are suddenly missing?"

"Oh, Rose!"

"Is there a name for it?"

"Incomplete." Caddy reached across and rubbed her little sister's drooping shoulders. "You would call it incomplete."

"Would you?"

"I think so. Is that how you felt when Tom went away?"

"Not at first," said Rose.

"The *coolest* name on the planet!"

Tom had said it again, the very last time that Rose had seen him. "*Permanent Rose!* Oh, yes! So what am I going to do without you, Permanent Rose?"

"You don't have to do without me."

"I have to go back to America."

"I'll still be here."

Indigo leaned over and scuffled Rose's hair with a music magazine he was holding. Tom did not reply at all, just grinned and bent a little lower over his guitar. There was a good feeling in the air, the way that happens in a place when all the people there are friends with each other. If Rose could have stopped time right then, she would have, but she couldn't. Time went on, and Tom went away.

This was how it had happened, that for Indigo and Rose, the summer began with an ending. Tom was gone. He had gone home to America because his baby sister was seriously ill. Earlier in the year he had fled to England to escape her. Now, it seemed, she might escape him instead.

Ever since the night Tom had left, Indigo and Rose had waited for news.

Hour by hour, and then day by day.

No news came.

Nothing.

Tom, comrade and companion-in-arms to Indigo,

troubadour, jester, and storyteller to Rose, sent no word at all.

He did not telephone, and he did not write. He did not communicate in any way. They had not heard a word from him.

It was not so bad for Indigo; he was older, and he had Tom's old guitar to learn to play, and he had a larger supply of patience than most people. He said, "Tom knows where we are. And it hasn't been that long."

It seemed long to Rose. The summer holidays had passed in a blur of heat and waiting. Tom's absence haunted her. In town she would catch glimpses of someone with a walk like his, and for a moment be certain that he was back. At night she often dreamed of him, stifling nightmares of noncommunication. Two or three times she struggled right out of these dreams and down the stairs to the kitchen, convinced she had heard the telephone ring.

"It is two o'clock in the morning, Rose!" said Eve, hugging her, the third time this happened. "And anyway, we cannot even hear the telephone upstairs, unless all the doors are open."

"I know."

"Come on back to bed then. You should be asleep."

"Can we leave all the doors open?"

"Do you fall asleep waiting for the telephone to ring, Rose?"

Rose nodded.

"No wonder you have nightmares," said Eve, but after that all the doors were left open, and Rose's nightmares stopped.

The nightmares stopped, but Rose's waiting did not stop. She still jumped every time the telephone rang, or when she saw a familiar gray jacket in the street. She waited impatiently for the post every morning.

"Do you know how long Tom has been gone *now*?" she asked Indigo that last Monday morning of the summer holidays.

"It must be more than five weeks."

"It has been five weeks and two days," said Rose.

"Oh."

"Five weeks, two days, and about eleven hours. Why are you smiling?"

"Because your math is so good."

"It wasn't math, it was counting," said Rose.

• • •

When David rang the doorbell of Indigo's house, Tom had been gone five weeks and two days and about twelve hours.

At the sound of the bell Rose jumped. Something inside her lifted, and then dropped a little too far. As if her heart had unexpectedly missed a step on a stairway.

She rushed to the door and dragged it open, but of course it was not Tom. It was only David, smelling (as usual) of sweets and sweat and looking redder and hotter than it was natural for any human being to look, even in the middle of a heat wave.

Rose gazed at him with dislike, which did not upset David because he did not notice.

"I've come to see Indigo," he announced.

"He's in the garden," snapped Rose, and shut the door as quickly as she had pulled it open.

David was never very fast at taking in information, especially when it was hurled at him by white-faced little girls with hardly any clothes on. So he remained where he was, huge, sticky, panting a little, and he was still there when Rose pulled the door open again and demanded, "Would you like to be tattooed?"

"Yes," said David, who longed more than anything to be tattooed, pierced, studded, thin, witty, swift, and effortlessly cool, and was none of these things.

"Oh, good."

Then David noticed that Rose was holding a bunch of ballpoint pens in one hand and an old-fashioned steel-nibbed pen in the other, that various parts of her body were beautifully patterned in red and blue ink, and that she was looking speculatively at his own large, pink unadorned arms.

"I've been practicing designs all week," he heard her say. "And I've just found this pen, and I'm sure it's sharp enough to do the real thing. . . . I don't suppose it hurts much . . . Come back!"

But David had already gone, fleeing in horror around the side of the house, past the overgrown fig tree whose dark leaves rubbed and rustled as if there were animals among them, and across to the patch of rough grass and guinea-pig hutches that the Casson family called a garden.

Rose should have called, "Stop!"—thus saving him. But she didn't.